BOYFRIEND
FOR THE
holidays

MM Short Story Romance

GAIA TATE

© Copyright 2024 by Gaia Tate. All rights reserved.

The characters and events portrayed in this book are fictitious. Any similarity to real persons, living or dead, is coincidental and not intended by the author.

No part of this book may be reproduced, or stored in a retrieval system, or transmitted in any form or by any means, electronic, mechanical, photocopying, recording, or otherwise, without express written permission of the author.

Copyright © 2024 by Gaia Tate
FIC027190

TikTok @authorgaiatate
Instagram @authorgaiatate
E-mail authorgaiatate@gmail.com

Chapter 1
The Boyfriend Act

I sit on the edge of my bed, staring down pensively at the half-packed suitcase lying open on the floor. Each item I've carefully placed inside feels like a part of some strange ritual—an attempt to prepare myself for a holiday I'm not even sure I want to face.

Christmas is just days away, and with it comes the annual pressures of family expectations. Every year, it's the same routine—show up alone and endure the endless questions, the disappointed glances from my mom and dad, and my grandmother's relentless matchmaking attempts. At twenty-eight, I'm just tired of it all. Tired of never meeting their expectations, tired of disappointing everyone, tired of disappointing myself.

This year, for the first time, I wonder if I might just stay home. I sigh, running a hand slowly through my hair, feeling the weight of my family's expectations settle over me like a thick winter coat.

My parents have a very specific vision of a "successful" Christmas—the whole family crammed together like a modern-day Noah's Ark, two-by-two, everyone paired off and accounted for. I can practically hear my mother's delighted coos as she admires the perfect pairs: my sister and her husband with their two little children, my brother and his pregnant wife. But her joy always shifts to a thinly veiled disappointment, almost pity, when her gaze lands on the empty chair beside me.

My dad, a practical guy, measures success through tangible achievements, expressing his disappointment with those long, loaded silences and shared looks with my mom. He never asks about my love life, but he gives me this look, like some prophet who can already see me destined to die alone. Accepting that I'm gay hasn't been easy for him—not because he's homophobic, but because he knows having kids won't be straightforward for me. For some reason, he seems convinced that if I'm not out there accidentally knocking up a random girl, I'll never actually go through the trouble of having kids at all. And maybe he's not wrong, but that's the last thing I want to worry about.

Then there are my siblings—my sister, a stay-at-home mom of two, practically a fixture in our parents' lives, married to a rich husband who makes working optional, and my older brother, with his high-paying finance job, loving wife, and a baby on the way—the picture of stability. Their lives only seem to spotlight my own shortcomings, so every time I sit at the table with them, I feel like I'm wading through the same swamp, year after year, with nothing to show for myself. We only see each other on holidays, and although we message a couple of times a week, the Big Questions are saved for our face-to-face moments—because it's just easier to torture me and watch my reaction in real time.

With another sigh, I lie back on the bed, frustration creeping in. Maybe I could skip the holiday this year. I could call my mom, claim that work is keeping me busy (a bold-faced lie, considering my assistant editor gig at an indie publishing house mostly involves reading manuscripts from the slush pile—and she knows it), or maybe say I've come down with the flu. Not a huge stretch, considering my scratchy throat, but I got a flu shot back in September and would never admit to my parents that it didn't work, especially since I'm still on my mission to convince them to get theirs annually. Besides, if I don't show up, I'll become the holiday's hot topic, and Mom will definitely cook up her own theory about what's "really" wrong with me. So, not going isn't really an option for me.

My phone buzzes on the nightstand, yanking me out of my spiraling thoughts. It's a message from Kelly, my best friend since high school.

Kelly: Hey! Are we still on for coffee?

I quickly type back, grateful for the distraction.

Mitch: Definitely. I could use some caffeine and your unsolicited advice. When?

Kelly: 30 mins, the Rabbit Hole?

Mitch: Okaaay, let's go!

Over the years, we've shared everything—secrets, heartbreaks, and countless late-night talks about love, life, and all the chaos in between. Kelly was the one who helped me come out, even standing by my side when I did it in front of my parents. She was there when my first boyfriend, who I'd been obsessed with for three years, dumped me; she was there again when my second boyfriend cheated on me. And I've been there for her too, through her own boyfriend's betrayal, the infamous "HPV-gate" (our name for her six-month ordeal of doctor visits, cervical dysplasia, and cancer scare, all thanks to the HPV her boyfriend passed along), and her rocky distance from her mom. Kelly is my bestie, my number one, my go-to girl.

Less than thirty minutes later, I'm sitting across from her at our favorite coffee shop, the Rabbit Hole. It's a cozy spot halfway between our places, with soft lighting, a minimalist Scandinavian design with marble and wood surfaces, and the warm aroma of fresh coffee and berry-jam-filled pastries.

"So, when are you leaving?" Kelly asks, biting into her cherry puff and scattering crumbs on her plate, the table, and her lap.

"Christmas Day. I thought about just coming for dinner to avoid all the prep, but Jemma swore she'd kill me if I skipped out on the hassle."

Kelly smirks. "Of course she did. So, staying a couple of days as usual?"

I nod. "I took a week off, but I don't want to overstay. Once the Christmas glow fades and everyone else leaves, it's just me, Mom, Dad, and Grandma, and that's when they start the find-pathetic-Mitch-a-boyfriend routine."

"Oh, come on," Kelly teases, taking a gulp of coffee. "It's not too bad if they start matchmaking again and set you up with one of the neighbors' sons, like last year." With her glossy black hair in two braids, dark eyeliner, and pale skin courtesy of her face powder, she looks like a Chinese-American Wednesday Addams.

"Are you kidding?" I nearly spit my coffee. "That was one of the most humiliating nights of my life. Need a refresher?"

Kelly laughs, holding her hands up defensively. "No need, I remember. So what if it was an awkward date in front of the family—"

"Kells, he was forty."

"You're 28; it's not that huge of a gap."

"I was twenty-seven."

"Tomeito, tomahto."

"He was bald!"

Kelly cracks up, almost spilling her coffee. "Oh, right! But he wasn't *completely* bald. He was bal*ding*. There's a difference."

I roll my eyes. "Tomeito, tomahto."

We laugh in unison.

Kelly and I are opposites. Where I'm reserved and introspective, she's bold and spontaneous. Her knack for finding silver linings often pulls us into impulsive adventures that make me question my cautious approach to life. But every time I try spontaneity—like agreeing to meet Mrs. Dwindle's balding, Star Wars–clueless accountant son—it reminds me why some of us (like yours truly) aren't meant for wild spontaneity.

After we finish our pastries and coffee, Kelly sets her cup down, her expression shifting from thoughtful to suddenly excited, like she's just had a brilliant idea.

"You know," she begins, a glimmer of mischief in her eyes, "you could easily solve this whole thing with your family. Just... bring someone."

I raise an eyebrow, sensing she has something up her sleeve. "You're offering to come with me?"

Kelly shakes her head. "No, dummy. You know I can't. My mom would never let me skip Christmas. Plus, I meant, bring a boyfriend."

I sigh dramatically. "Oh, thanks, Kells! Why didn't I think of that? My imaginary boyfriend is dying to meet my family!"

Kelly snorts. "Stop with the sass. I'm serious."

"Alright," I shrug. "But you know, I don't have a boyfriend, right?"

A grin spreads across her face. "Well, if it's just to get through the holidays," she says slyly, "why not find a 'boyfriend for hire'?"

I blink, surprised by her suggestion. "You mean...pay someone to pretend to be my boyfriend?"

She shrugs, leaning back but keeping her gaze on me. "Why not? And I happen to know someone who'd be perfect for the job."

I give her a skeptical look, but despite myself, there's this strange flicker of excitement mixed with anxiety bubbling in my chest. I don't even know what this feeling is, but Kelly has a talent for shaking up my boring life. I'm instantly anxious but also curious. "Like who?"

"How about Garred?" Kelly suggests, a wicked glint in her eye. "My flat mate, remember? He's charming, easy to talk to, and could totally play the perfect boyfriend for your family."

I raise an eyebrow, completely baffled. "Garred the firefighter? Are you kidding me?"

Garred the firefighter is, hands down, the hottest guy I've ever seen. He's tall, dark-haired, and built like a mountain of lean muscle, with that brooding look of a young Hollywood actor. When I first met him, I seriously considered starting a small fire at my house just so he'd come rescue me.

Kelly laughs. "Why not? He's hot, charming, great with parents, and my mom practically adores him."

"You want me to take your boyfriend to meet my family?" I say, dumbfounded.

"He's *not* my boyfriend," Kelly says, her expression faltering just for a second before she quickly masks it with a smile.

"What if you guys start dating? How am I supposed to explain that to my family?"

"That's not going to happen," she says firmly.

"Didn't you have a crush on him or something?" I ask, frowning.

"Not anymore," Kelly says. "He's out of my league."

I squint at her suspiciously. "Since when? Weren't you planning to hook up with him on New Year's by getting him drunk?"

Kelly blushes a bit but shakes her head. "Actually, we talked last week, and I realized I'm not his type."

I frown even more. "You're hiding something."

She shakes her head. "Nope."

Then something dawns on me. "Wait...is he gay?"

Kelly looks me dead in the eye. "Nope. Straight as an arrow."

I blush, embarrassed by the flicker of hope I let myself feel, and let out a frustrated sigh. Kelly never hides anything from me, and now she's obviously holding something back. But I'm too rattled to press her now. I'll pry it out of her once I get back from the holiday.

"Alright," I say, "but what makes you think he'd even agree to something like this? Isn't he, like, super serious?"

"Nah," Kelly says, finishing her coffee. "He's actually pretty cool. We've become really close friends."

"Since when?!"

Kelly ignores my question, brushing it off. "I'll just call him right now and ask."

I hesitate, turning the idea over in my mind. Then, feeling a sudden wave of bravery, I nod. "You're crazy," I tell her as she grins, unfazed, and pulls out her phone.

"Let's see what he says."

In the next second, she's dialing him. I watch, slightly stunned, as she puts the call on speaker. A moment later, Garred's deep, smooth voice comes through, as confident as if he's always winning at life—the guy has serious Henry Cavill energy.

"Hey, Kelly! What's up? Did you forget your keys again?"

"Nope, Gar. I'm here with Mitch, and you're on speaker!" she replies, as casual as if they've been friends for years.

"Hey, Mitch," Garred says, his voice a low rumble, and I feel something flip in my stomach. Oh god. *This was a terrible idea.*

"Hey," I mumble, suddenly desperate to make Kelly drop this whole thing.

But before I can start wildly gesturing for her to stop, Kelly blurts out, "Quick question: how would you feel about playing the role of Mitch's boyfriend for a weekend? Just to help him out with his family over the holidays."

There's a brief pause on the other end, during which I think I might actually self-combust, before Garred laughs. "Playing Mitch's boyfriend, huh?" he says, amused. "On Christmas? Are we going for a Hallmark vibe here?"

"Sort of," Kelly says, unfazed. "Mitch needs help because his family thinks he's a total loser who'll die alone," she adds, and I slap my forehead with my palm as she throws in, "and he can pay you a hundred bucks."

A hundred bucks?! A heads-up would be nice, but whatever.

I tense, waiting for Garred's answer, looking at Kelly in horror.

Garred laughs again, deep and warm. I hold my breath, praying he's about to say no.

"Sure, why not," Garred says suddenly. "I didn't have any plans for Christmas anyway."

I feel my face heat up, half in shock, half in horror, as I wonder if he's serious. Kelly seems to think the same because she asks, "Are you serious?"

"Yeah," Garred says, casual as anything. "And I don't need the hundred bucks. Just feed me some homemade meals, and we'll call it even."

"Thank you, Garred! You're the best!" Kelly beams at me. "Talk soon! Bye!" She hangs up and turns to me with a triumphant grin. "See? I told you he'd be perfect!"

I nod, still a little dazed by what just happened and what I've signed up for. My mind is already racing, picturing all the ways this could go wrong. Each one of my overactive fantasies basically looks like a scene from *Meet the Fockers*—pure disaster, just with a lot more family chaos. I feel a tiny bit of relief, though, remembering that at least Grandma's still around, so we won't have any accidental urn incidents.

Kelly squirms with excitement. "Yaaay! You've got yourself a boyfriend for the holidays!"

Oh god.

What have I gotten myself into?

Chapter 2
The Road Home

The small plane's engine hums steadily as it cuts through the wintry sky, soaring over an endless expanse of snow-dusted trees and frozen lakes below. I glance out the window, watching the landscape slip away beneath us.

Garred, Kelly's flat mate and my "boyfriend" for the weekend, looks totally at ease beside me. With all his muscle, broad shoulders, sharp jawline, and mesmerizing dark eyes, he looks like he belongs in a fantasy novel, not cramped beside me on this tiny plane.

We've been airborne for about an hour and a half, mostly making polite small talk. Garred's been absorbed in a Brandon Sanderson novel, occasionally glancing at me or out the window. We briefly discussed our charade last night when I joined him and Kelly at their apartment, but now I get the feeling Garred's expecting me to lay out some huge master plan, like we're about to pull an *Ocean's Twelve* con. But the truth is, I don't have a plan. Not really.

"Feels like we're headed straight into a holiday postcard," Garred says, his voice cutting through the hum of the cabin.

He glances out the window, a half-smile forming as he takes in the snowy forests below.

"Yeah," I reply, a bit stiffly. "It's...pretty remote."

Garred nods and turns to look at me with those piercing dark eyes. He really does look like Henry Cavill. Maybe even better—if that's possible. "So," he says, leaning back in his chair, "not that I'm complaining, but how did I end up being your holi-date?"

I blush up to my ears, cheeks now matching my red Christmas sweater, and fumble a little under his steady gaze. "Uh," I say, "my family loves torturing me about my lack of a boyfriend every year, and I...well, Kelly suggested bringing a fake one."

Garred raises an eyebrow. "So you don't have a boyfriend?"

Is he surprised? Or is he teasing? I can't tell.

"Obviously not," I mutter, chewing my lip and looking anywhere but at him.

"Why 'obviously'?" he asks, his gaze lingering. "You've got this cute puppy thing going on."

"I—uh..." I get so flustered I lose the ability to speak. "I just meant 'obviously' because I asked you—" I trail off, my face burning.

Garred laughs, deep and easy, clearly enjoying my discomfort. "So, what are the rules?" he asks after a pause, tapping the armrest thoughtfully. "For our little act, I mean."

I feel myself flush again, both from his question and the realization that we haven't set any ground rules. "Just...keep it casual. My family's going to ask a lot of questions, so be ready. And, um, feel free to improvise."

"Noted," Garred says, his eyes twinkling. "So, if I say I saved you from a burning building, they'll believe that?"

"Maybe not that," I reply, a small, reluctant smile tugging at my lips. "But we could say we met through Kelly. That part's true, at least."

Garred nods, his gaze flickering back to me. "So, Kelly's the matchmaker. Anything else?"

I hesitate, feeling suddenly self-conscious. "You might have to...you know, act a bit affectionate."

He raises an eyebrow, smirking. "I can handle that." His voice is light, but there's something intense in his eyes that makes my heart beat faster. "What exactly are we talking? Hugs? Holding hands? Pecks on the cheek?"

"Yeah," I nod, hoping the poor lighting in the plane hides how flustered I am.

"Kisses?" Garred asks, and I freeze, my heart pounding loudly in my chest, before he continues with a completely straight face, "Sex?"

I choke on my own saliva, erupting into a coughing fit so violent that Garred starts to look embarrassed, telling me it was just a joke. But I'm too far gone, my windpipe waging war with my dignity as other passengers turn to look and a flight attendant hurries over, asking if I'm okay. As soon as I manage to stop coughing, I assure her I'm fine, but she still brings me a glass of water. I gulp it down, not daring to look at Garred.

"Sorry," he says, giving me an apologetic look. "That was a dumb joke."

"It's fine," I say, trying to salvage the last drops of my dignity. "It wasn't about that. It's just the dry air...always makes me cough."

Garred nods, but I know he doesn't buy it.

Thankfully, at that exact moment, the plane dips lower, and the captain turns on the seatbelt sign, signaling our final descent. I exhale in relief, grateful for the distraction.

My nerves are in overdrive, and Garred's calm confidence isn't exactly helping.

As the plane begins its descent, I focus on the landscape below: winding roads, clusters of snow-dusted evergreens, and cozy houses scattered across the hills. Garred glances out the window, looking mildly curious and completely at ease, while my pulse quickens with a mix of anticipation and anxiety.

A quarter of an hour later, the wheels touch down, and soon we're stepping off the plane into the brisk winter air. It hits me sharply, reminding me we're now in my hometown, where the snow is thicker and the cold is sharper. The small airport bustles quietly, filled with travelers bundled in winter coats, making holiday plans in hushed tones.

Garred doesn't hesitate, grabbing my heavy bag off the luggage carousel like it weighs nothing. I didn't bring much for myself, but I have gifts for everyone. We head toward the rental car area, and my nerves start to hum again. I take a deep breath, trying to steady myself, but my pulse only seems to quicken.

"You alright?" Garred asks, noticing my nerves.

"Yeah, sorry," I say, "I'm just nervous this whole idea might be a little dumb. No offense."

"I'm not going to embarrass you or anything, don't worry." Garred smiles confidently, and I believe him.

We load our bags into the trunk—Garred only has a backpack—and he slides into the driver's seat, giving me a small, amused smile as he adjusts the mirrors. I climb in, feeling both the weight and anticipation of what lies ahead.

After a few miles winding through snowy roads, Garred breaks the silence, glancing at me. "So," he says casually, "since I'm supposed to be your boyfriend, I should probably know a little more about you."

I let out a laugh, relieved by the change in tone. "Yeah, probably a good idea."

"Alright," he prompts. "What should I know?"

I take a breath, gathering my thoughts. "I'm an assistant editor. I work at Herrey's. I read manuscripts from unpublished writers."

"Yeah, Kelly told me about that," Garred says, nodding as he focuses on the road. "How do you usually spend your evenings?"

I shrug, a little embarrassed. "Uh, I don't know, like...play computer games or something."

"Nice," Garred says approvingly. "What do you play?"

"*Rome: Total War. Age of Empires II.*"

Garred frowns. "Aren't those, like, a hundred years old?"

I snort. "They're classics, thank you very much. They don't get old."

"Yeah, if you like shuffling pixels around," Garred laughs.

"How dare you! They were *remastered*."

He throws a grin my way. "I'm just messing with you. I like those games too. Been playing *Warhammer: Total War* for, like, a year straight."

I blink at him. "Wait, seriously?"

Garred nods. "Yup."

"You're not just saying that, right? I can't tell if you're messing with me."

He raises an eyebrow. "Why would I mess with you?"

I stammer, "You just don't seem like...a gamer."

He smirks. "Don't judge a book by its cover, Mitchell."

"Don't call me Mitchell," I say, blushing. "Nobody calls me that."

"Should I call you 'sunshine' then?" he says, cocking an eyebrow. "We're supposed to have nicknames, right? Or how about 'sweetcheeks'?"

I snort. "God, you're insufferable." But I'm already feeling a bit more at ease, though the warmth in my belly isn't exactly going away.

Garred glances over, amused. "Kelly warned me you're not the romantic type. So try to work on that, or your family might not buy this."

"Kelly said *what*?" I blurt out, turning to him in disbelief. "She doesn't know anything!"

"Isn't she, like, your best friend?"

"She is, but...she doesn't know anything," I repeat, feeling the sudden need to have a little chat with Kelly. I glance out the window, snow-covered pines stretching out like a frosty winter postcard.

"So," Garred says, bringing me back. "How should I be addressing you?"

"Mitch is fine," I say.

He rolls his eyes. "Real couples don't use government names. If we were actually dating, I wouldn't call you Mitch."

"Oh yeah? So what would you call me?" I ask, a bit dumbstruck.

He doesn't hesitate. "Baby."

I look away, my face burning and mutter, "Alright."

We ride in silence for a few minutes until I break it. "We should come up with a code phrase. A signal, in case things get weird."

"A code phrase?" Garred frowns, puzzled. "Like what?"

"Like, 'can I have a word with you' if I need us to leave the room."

Garred raises an eyebrow. "Isn't that a pretty normal phrase?"

"Exactly. But if I say it, it means we need to leave the room for an actual talk."

He looks amused but nods. "Alright, got it. I'll be on high alert for that."

I manage a nod, feeling a little less tense. It's good to know we're on the same page, even if I still feel slightly ridiculous for needing a "code phrase" in the first place.

As we drive through the winding road, the landscape shifts from untouched wilderness to the cozy beginnings of the village. Snow blankets every rooftop and tree branch, creating a winter scene lit up by tiny holiday lights on houses and lampposts. My pulse quickens—my family's house is only a few miles away, waiting with all the warmth (and scrutiny) that comes with the season.

Sensing my nerves, Garred reaches over and gives my shoulder a reassuring squeeze. "Relax. Moms love me."

"So I've heard," I say, feeling my skin tingle under his touch, even through my thick coat and sweater. Well, sort of. "I just hope she doesn't love you *too* much, or I'll get jealous." The words slip out before I can stop them. I clear my throat, silently praying he didn't catch that slip-up.

Garred seems to let it slide, or maybe he didn't notice. After a moment of silence, he asks, "So, you're okay with touching, right?"

"Yeah," I reply as casually as I can muster, but my calm almost crumbles when his hand moves from my shoulder to my cheek in a gentle caress. I must be blushing like crazy because even that small touch sends a spark through me. God, I could actually melt from this.

He gives a thoughtful nod and then drops his hand. "Looks like I'll have my work cut out for me."

I laugh nervously, trying to ignore the warm flush spreading over my cheeks. I'm not entirely sure I'm ready for what's about to happen.

The town comes into view, each house strung with lights and wreaths, the perfect small-town holiday postcard. As we pass by, I feel a strange mix of comfort and anxiety. I glance at Garred, who's focused on the road, calm and steady.

Finally, five minutes later, we turn onto the driveway leading to my family's home. The old stone house is nestled among the trees, its windows glowing warmly against the snowy backdrop. Twinkling lights line the roof and windows, casting a soft glow over the front yard. I hear faint Christmas music drifting out, mingling with the crunch of snow under the tires.

Garred parks and looks over at me, smirking. "Well, here we are. Ready, baby?"

I take a shaky breath, looking toward the house. "As ready as I'll ever be."

We step out of the car, the cold biting at my cheeks as we walk down the snowy path to the front door. Through the window, I can see my family bustling around the kitchen, probably already knee-deep in holiday prep.

Garred falls into step beside me, and his presence is surprisingly steadying. As we approach the door, I glance up, feeling a surge of gratitude I hadn't expected.

"Just know," I say quietly, "they're probably going to jump on us the second we walk in."

Garred chuckles, his breath misting in the cold air. "I've got you. Relax, baby."

I nod, heart pounding as we reach the doorstep. I hate how much I love the way he says "baby." But then he takes my hand, lifting it to his lips to place a quick kiss on my palm. I feel myself melting on the spot.

Taking one last deep breath, I open the door, and we're instantly enveloped by the warmth and light inside. The air fills with Christmas music, laughter, and the comforting scent of homemade holiday food.

Chapter 3
Meet the Family

"Mom, Dad," I call out as soon as the door closes behind us, and we're enveloped by the warmth of the house and the mouthwatering smells drifting from the kitchen.

No one seems to hear me over the music and the chaos coming from the dining room, where, judging by the noise, Jemma's kids are shrieking and running around, their little footsteps thumping against the floor.

I glance at Garred, who has already set down the bags, shrugged off his coat, and hung it on the rack by the door. Now, he's silently offering to help me with my coat. I let him, and as he eases it off my shoulders, my mom walks out of the kitchen, her back to us. Just in time for the show.

"Mom," I say, and she turns, freezing as she takes us in.

"Mitch, honey, you're here!" She flutters her hands and rushes to hug me, though her utterly surprised gaze is fixed on Garred. It's clear she didn't expect to see a Greek god standing next to her younger son.

I'd told her I'd be bringing a *friend*—yes, I said friend, just in case Garred backed out at the last minute, which would've left me scrambling to find a stand-in. So I imagine she's a little shocked to see a Henry Cavill lookalike at my side.

"And who's your friend?" Mom asks as she releases me.

"Mom," I start, my voice catching. I clear my throat. "This is, uh—"

"Garred," he steps in smoothly, flashing her an easy, Hollywood-worthy smile. "Mitch's boyfriend. It's wonderful to meet you, Mrs. Collins."

My mom just stares at him, clearly in shock. "B-boyfriend?" Her gaze darts to me, eyes full of questions, as though she can't believe I'd managed to bring home someone like Garred. I nod, trying to look as confident as possible.

"It's such a pleasure!" she exclaims, her voice cracking, and I can't believe how thrilled she seems that I've brought a guy home. She must have really lost hope if that's her reaction.

Garred, the towering figure that he is, leans down and wraps her in a hug, so genuine and warm that I'm actually a little annoyed it's all just part of the act for him. The hug seems to make my mom even more ecstatic; I swear I see tears welling in her eyes as she stands on tiptoe to hug him back. Kelly wasn't kidding—Garred really is a mom charmer.

As if to prove the point, as soon as he lets go, Garred sniffs the air and says, "Something smells amazing. Is that baked potatoes with rosemary I'm smelling, Mrs. Collins?"

My mom's face lights up like a Christmas tree. "Oh, yes! I'm trying out a new recipe, actually. And please, call me Linda."

Garred beams at her with his laser charm. "Linda, you have to share this recipe with me, or I'll be begging all night!"

Mom actually blushes—*blushes*—and gives me a look that practically screams, *where on Earth did you find him?* I can tell she's bursting with a million questions, but instead, she nearly bounces as she makes us take off our shoes and leads us toward the dining room.

As we walk in, she grabs my elbow and hisses—loud enough for Garred to hear—"Mitch, this is a Christmas miracle!"

Oh. My. God. My face heats up like a gas canister about to explode, and all I want to do right now is merge with the dining room floor like a chameleon. I glance at Garred, and he's clearly amused—he's smirking as if to say he's absolutely going to bring this up later, especially since my mom's reaction makes it sound like she'd given up on my dating life entirely.

I will myself to stop blushing, but then it hits me that my entire family isn't even here yet—meaning this is just the warm-up—and my face somehow heats up even more. Just then, Garred's hand finds the small of my back, as if he's trying to steady me. His touch feels like a brand through my sweater.

"You okay?" he murmurs, pulling me a bit closer and then wrapping his arms around my waist. His voice is soft, just for me, but I can see Mom sneaking glances from the doorway, her eyes practically starry.

"Yeah," I mutter, and to my surprise, Garred leans down and plants a quick kiss on my cheek. My skin burns where his lips touch, and when I look up at him, he's smiling—a warm, private smile that feels like it's meant just for my eyes. Except, of course, it's not, because Mom is right there.

Just then, my niece and nephew, covered head-to-toe in what looks suspiciously like glitter, finally spot me. They dart over, and Garred lets go so they can give me a quick hug. Then they turn their attention to Garred, staring up at him as if he's a superhero come to life. When he says hello, they let out high-pitched squeals and bolt out of the room, thrilled.

"Your dad and Adam went out to pick up Grandma," Mom says casually, but I can tell she's stalling to soak in every second of Garred's presence. She probably thinks he'll vanish into thin air if she looks away. "They'll be here soon."

"Great," I say, nodding, still feeling a bit overheated from Garred's proximity. "Where's everyone else?"

"In the kitchen, helping me finish up dinner."

"We'd be happy to help," Garred offers, but Mom waves him off, smiling warmly.

"Oh, no need, dear, there are already too many cooks." She beams at him. "Would you like something to drink? The mulled wine isn't quite ready yet, but we have champagne."

"We brought red wine," Garred replies smoothly, and I immediately start looking around for my bag. But before I can even think about going for it, he says, "I'll grab it," and heads into the hallway.

"That's so lovely of you," Mom says, clearly charmed, as Garred returns a moment later with two bottles. He places them on the family table in the middle of the room, already set with a white tablecloth, cutlery, glasses, plates, and neatly folded napkins.

Just then, Jemma walks into the dining room, saying, "Mom, the kids are convinced there's a Superma—" She stops abruptly, noticing Garred and me. "Oh. Hi."

"Hi, Jem," I say, moving over to give her a hug. I feel her stiffen a little, probably as she glances over my shoulder at Garred.

He steps forward, waiting politely until Jemma releases me. Then he says, "I'm Garred. It's great to finally meet you, Jemma."

I catch the word "finally" and can't help but appreciate the nice touch—Garred definitely knows how to make an impression. Jemma raises an eyebrow, glancing between the two of us.

"Wait, are you...?"

"Garred's my boyfriend," I say quickly, feeling his arm settle around my shoulders, his spicy, pine-scented cologne making me a bit lightheaded. I can't help but enjoy how we seem to fit together, like I'm a little missing puzzle piece nestled under his arm.

"I thought you were just bringing a friend," Jemma says, looking a bit thrown.

"Yeah," I say, aware of Garred's gaze on me, "I didn't want everyone to fuss."

"Well, we wouldn't fuss if we knew you had a boyfriend," Jemma says, giving me an offended look.

"I—" I start, but Garred steps in smoothly.

"Sorry, that's probably my fault. I was a bit nervous to meet everyone."

"Nervous?" Jemma repeats, a trace of suspicion in her voice.

"Yeah," Garred nods, and I could swear he's blushing a little. "I was just nervous I might not live up to the Collins family standards."

I stare at him, wondering if he's secretly a sociopath—he lies so smoothly and says exactly the right thing. Jemma immediately softens, giving him a warm smile.

"Trust me, we don't have any expectations when it comes to Mitch's boyfriends."

I want to slap myself in the face. "Thanks for that, Jem."

"What? It's true. You never bring any of your boyfriends to meet us, so we assume they don't exist."

Garred laughs at that, and Jemma joins in, though she sounds a bit offended, and I want to kick both of them for making me the punchline.

Jemma's not wrong, though. I've never brought anyone

home—my first serious boyfriend was way out of my league, and I spent most of our relationship fangirling over him. I did ask him to meet my parents once, but he always refused. With my second boyfriend, I didn't even bother trying. So, yeah, Jemma's got a point.

When Mom mentions something about potatoes and heads to the kitchen, I leave Garred and Jemma to their chat and head to the table to open the wine. I wrestle with the corkscrew for a moment before finally winning and pouring myself a glass—a generous pour that would easily be three servings in a restaurant. But if I'm going to make it through tonight without being a total awkward mess, I need a drink. So I finish the glass in less than two minutes and pour myself another.

As I sip my second glass, Adam's pregnant wife, Claire, comes in holding a dish with a lid, followed by Jemma's husband, Rick, who's carrying another covered dish. They appear so quickly after Mom left that I'd bet my yearly bonus she already filled them in about my "boyfriend," and now they're here to get a look. I watch them meet Garred while I finish my drink, and it's clear he's basically a Dale Carnegie when it comes to winning people over. As they laugh and chat, I feel a pang of annoyance—apparently, I'm not the only one getting Garred's full attention. But I also can't figure out why he's putting so much effort into this whole act. Maybe he'll be asking for that hundred bucks after all.

When everyone turns to look at me, sitting there with my wine glass, I realize I have no choice but to get up and hug my in-laws. And even though I'm genuinely happy to see them, I feel so awkward it's like my arms and legs are made of wood.

And, as if my limbs really are made of wood, I trip over the carpet.

"Shit!" I shout, but it's too late. I would've spilled my wine all over the floor if Garred hadn't caught me just in time, the wine landing on him instead of the pristine white carpet.

We freeze: me in Garred's arms, my wine glass nearly empty in my hand, and Garred's blue shirt now soaked in red. For a moment, time stands still—until it snaps back, and the whole family springs into action, hurrying over with paper towels and wet wipes. Mom hears the commotion from the kitchen, rushes in to see what happened, and, *thank god*, realizes the carpet is saved. She hurries back to the kitchen and returns with salt, explaining that Garred will need to take off his shirt to soak the stain before it sets.

And when Garred finally pulls off his shirt, revealing the sharp lines of his chest and abs, I feel the blood drain from my face like I spilled it along with the wine.

Fuck me, he looks good.

Before my mom can start fussing, I take Garred upstairs to the guest bathroom and leave him to clean up while I run to my old room to find one of my faded high-school T-shirts. When I come back, I stop short at the doorway—Garred is standing there in just his briefs, trying to blot the stain out of his pants. He glances at me, and I do my best not to stare as I say, "I'm so sorry, Garred. I'll cover the cost of the clothes."

He snorts, "Relax, it's fine."

I walk over, hand him the shirt, and eye the dark red stain on his pant leg. "I'll grab my sweatpants for you."

"The pants are fine," Garred says with an easy smile, hanging them on a hook by the mirror. I notice a bit of wine staining his stomach, so I pick up a fresh towel, wet it, and start dabbing the wine off his skin.

Garred chuckles, but when I reach the spot just above his briefs, he gently catches my wrist with a small smile. "It's fine, thank you."

"Oh—yeah, of course," I stammer, feeling incredibly awkward for touching him without thinking.

I back away, embarrassed, as Garred pulls his pants back on and then slips the borrowed T-shirt over his head. It's too small, stretching tight across his chest and shoulders, but at least it reaches his waist.

"Did you bring any spare clothes?" I ask. "I can run downstairs and grab your bag."

"Yeah, but don't worry about it. This is fine."

Before I can apologize for the wine again, there's a knock at the door.

"Everything okay in there?" Mom calls out, her voice tinged with concern.

"Fine!" I reply, a little too quickly. "We'll be right down!"

"Okay, dear. Your father, brother, and Grandma just arrived!"

Garred looks at me, amused, as he adjusts the shirt. "Ready to meet the rest of the family?"

"I need another drink," I mutter, running a hand through my hair.

"Hey," Garred says softly, catching my hand. "Deep breaths. You're doing great."

His touch is gentle as he draws slow circles on my wrist, and despite my embarrassment over the wine incident, I find myself calming down. He's right—aside from my clumsiness, things are actually going surprisingly well. My family seems totally charmed by him, which is both a relief and oddly unsettling.

"Thanks," I say, managing a small smile. "And sorry again about your clothes."

"Stop apologizing," he says, giving my hand a squeeze before letting go. "Though I have to admit, this wasn't exactly how I pictured stripping down in front of you for the first time, baby."

I blush and laugh despite myself, feeling the tension ease completely. "Well, at least you made an impression on my family."

"That's one way to put it," he grins, then gestures at the exit. "Shall we?"

I nod, taking one last deep breath before opening the door. As we head downstairs, I can hear my grandmother's voice floating up from below, along with my father's deeper tone. Garred's hand finds the small of my back again, steadying me, and I try to ignore how natural it feels.

As we descend the stairs, my grandmother's voice gets clearer. She's talking about her bridge club's Christmas party drama—apparently someone brought store-bought cookies and tried to pass them off as homemade. The scandal.

When we reach the bottom step, Dad spots us first. He's helping Grandma with her coat, but his hands freeze mid-motion as he takes in the sight of Garred and me. His eyebrows shoot up so high they nearly disappear into his hairline. Judging by his reaction, mom had already called him and told him about Garred, but Dad probably didn't expect to see this muscled man by my side with whom we could easily cosplay Beauty and the Beast.

Then I notice Adam, and his reaction I was probably dreading even more than Dad's.

Adam looks like he's just stumbled onto a prank show. His eyes dart between Garred and me, clearly trying to process what he's seeing. I can practically hear the gears turning as he sizes up Garred's impressive height and build, currently showcased by my too-tight high school T-shirt, and then glances at me, his shorter, bookish younger brother.

"Well," Adam finally says, a hint of amusement in his voice, "this is...unexpected."

Before I can respond, Grandma pushes past both Dad and Adam, her eyes lighting up as she spots Garred. "Oh my!" she exclaims, shuffling forward. "And who do we have here?"

Garred steps forward smoothly, taking her outstretched hand in both of his. "I'm Garred, ma'am. Mitch's boyfriend. It's such a pleasure to meet you."

"Boyfriend!" Grandma practically squeals, holding onto Garred's hands. "Mitchell, you've been holding out on us!" She turns back to Garred, patting his arm approvingly. "And such a handsome one, too! I was starting to worry about our Mitchell. All those dating apps these days, and he still couldn't find anyone!"

"Grandma," I groan, but she just waves me off.

"Now, now, dear. Let me enjoy this moment." She beams up at Garred. "You have to tell me everything. How did you two meet?"

"Through a mutual friend," Garred replies smoothly.

"Kelly introduced us," I add quickly.

"Kelly?" Dad finally speaks up, his eyebrows still somewhere near his hairline. "Your friend from high school?"

I nod, grateful as Garred continues smoothly, "Yes, sir. I'm actually her roommate. Mitch and I met on Halloween."

That part, at least, is true.

"Halloween?" Adam repeats, doing the math in his head, then raises an eyebrow, a hint of skepticism in his voice. "*This* Halloween?"

I know exactly what he's implying—that I've brought a random fling to Christmas dinner with the family. But before I can decide how to respond, Garred flashes him a broad smile.

"Yeah, I'm a little embarrassed to admit it, but after one conversation, I was pretty much in love with him."

I blush (yes, I know, I do that a lot—don't judge), and Mom lets out an audible "aww." I catch Jemma and Rick exchanging surprised glances, clearly charmed by whatever Garred says. It hits me that they're all hanging onto his every word—everyone, that is, except Adam, who just smirks.

Funny enough, my first (and one of only a few) real conversations with Garred was completely ridiculous. I'd gone to pick up Kelly on Halloween, dressed as Edward Cullen (she was Alice Cullen), secretly hoping to get a glimpse of her new roommate. Garred had just finished his shift and was still in his firefighter uniform, covered in soot, which I naturally assumed was a brilliant costume. So, of course, I launched into this whole analysis about why firefighters wouldn't stand a chance against Twilight vampires. Garred just stood there, smiling and letting me ramble for a solid ten minutes until Kelly finally stepped in to tell me it wasn't a costume—he was actually a firefighter who'd just come off work.

I smile at the memory. Part of me wants to tell my family the story—it'd probably win Dad over in a second, considering he's always joked I'd never find someone patient enough to listen to my geeky rambles. But something about Adam's smirk makes me want to keep that moment to myself. It's too precious, too awkward, too real to hand over as proof against whatever cynical point Adam's trying to make about my love life.

"We'll see how it goes," Adam says with one of his deadpan smirks.

My brother isn't a bad person, but he's always been overprotective of me—in that annoying way where he tortures me instead of anyone else. When he found out I was gay, he went through a phase of believing older men would take advantage of me and gave me grief for a couple of months, until Dad got involved and told him to back off.

"Welcome to our home, Garred," Dad finally says as he steps forward, extending his hand.

Garred shakes it firmly. "Thank you for having me, sir."

"Yes, yes," Grandma cuts in impatiently. "But tell me more about how you two got together. Mitchell never tells us anything!"

Garred gives me a quick look at the use of "Mitchell," but I just stare back, making it clear that only Grandma is allowed to call me by my full name.

"Later, Grams," I tell her. Just then, Mom's phone timer goes off, and she announces, "Dinner's ready! Everyone to the table! I'll bring out the turkey and potatoes."

As we all move toward the dining room, I catch Adam giving me a look that clearly says we'll be talking later. But before I can start worrying about it, Garred's hand slips into mine, giving it a reassuring squeeze. The gesture feels so natural that, for a moment, I almost forget this is all pretend.

While Garred and I were upstairs, Mom decorated the dining table with a centerpiece of pine branches and red candles. She really outdid herself—everything looks like it belongs on the cover of a Christmas magazine.

"Garred, dear, why don't you sit next to Mitch?" Mom suggests, though we'd obviously do that anyway. "And Margaret," she says, glancing at Grandma, "why don't you sit on Garred's other side?"

I suppress a groan. Of course Mom would put Grandma next to Garred. She's probably hoping Grandma will pry every detail of our "relationship" out of him over dinner for later discussion. Grandma's a pro at that, and I'm already worried Garred won't survive the interrogation.

As we take our seats, I notice Garred's borrowed T-shirt ride up slightly when he sits, revealing a strip of skin at his waist. I quickly look away, but not before catching Jemma's knowing smirk from across the table.

"So, Garred," Dad says as Mom begins passing around the dishes, "what do you do for work?"

"I'm a firefighter, sir."

The table falls quiet for a moment, and I can practically see everyone's estimation of Garred rising even higher. Perfect. Now he's not just gorgeous—he's also a hero who saves lives.

"A firefighter!" Grandma exclaims, clasping her hands together. "How exciting! And dangerous too, I imagine. Mitchell, don't you worry about him?"

I nearly choke on my water. "I—uh—"

"I always make sure to let him know I'm safe," Garred cuts in smoothly, placing his hand over mine on the table.

The warmth of his hand sends a tingle up my arm, and when I glance at him, the soft look he's giving me feels almost too real, sending a storm of butterflies through my stomach.

"That's so sweet," Mom sighs, and I catch Jemma rolling her eyes with a good-natured smile.

As the food makes its way around, the questions keep coming, but Garred handles them all with effortless charm. Between questions, he compliments Mom's cooking, asks Dad about his work, coos at photos of Jemma's kids in their kindergarten play, and listens attentively to Grandma's bridge club stories. He's so perfect it's almost suspicious, but everyone is completely won over. Well, again, everyone except Adam.

"So, are you two like...casual, or what's going on here?" Adam asks, looking between the two of us.

"Adam!" Mom says, her brows furrowed. "What's gotten into you today?"

"I'm just asking," Adam says with a shrug, but of course, he's not "just asking."

"Yeah, right," I mutter, feeling a flash of anger rise in me.

"I'm not sure about Mitch, but I'm pretty serious," Garred says with a light laugh, though his hand squeezes my thigh under the table, a quiet contrast to his casual tone.

"Aren't all firefighters gay?" Adam says, earning a collective gasp around the table.

"Stop it, Adam," Claire says, poking him in the ribs. "You're embarrassing yourself."

"What?" Adam smirks, looking unapologetic. "I'm just asking."

I want to unleash hell on my brother, but Garred doesn't let me; his grip on my leg tightens under the table as he responds, this time without a smile. "I don't see where you're going with this."

Adam twists his mouth into a lopsided smirk. "I was just wondering why a guy like you would choose my brother, that's all. Aren't there enough hot guys around you?"

"You're being rude, Adam," Dad interjects, but Garred nods at him, signaling that he's got it, and then turns back to Adam.

"I'm not interested in dating a copy of myself, if that's what you're asking," Garred replies, with a smile that's anything but warm. "I get that you're being protective of your brother, and I respect that—especially since I'm in your family's home. But your questions are upsetting Mitch. All you need to know is that I'm in love with your brother. That should be enough."

Garred's reply puts Adam firmly in his place. Adam just shrugs and, for the rest of dinner, doesn't bring it up again. The way Garred handled it clearly earned him points with the rest of my family—and with me, too. For the first time, I felt like I caught a glimpse of the real Garred, someone not quite so perfect, a little territorial even, which, I'll admit, I liked a little too much.

Chapter 4
Heat

After the confrontation with Adam settles, dinner continues at a more relaxed pace. The tension gradually dissolves as Mom brings out her traditional Christmas sides—the honey-glazed carrots, her special cranberry sauce, and the green bean casserole that's been part of our family dinners since before I can remember. Garred tries everything, making appreciative noises that have Mom practically glowing with pride. He then actually asks her for that potato recipe and even writes it down in his phone. I'm not sure if Garred is truly a food enthusiast, but he seems genuinely excited to have this recipe, especially since, as he put it himself, he "had at least three servings" of the said potatoes and didn't go for a fourth one just out of manners.

While they chat, I'm picking at my carrots, still a bit unsettled by Adam's comments, when I feel Garred's leg press against mine under the table. It's subtle, probably meant to be reassuring, but it sends a wave of warmth through me that has nothing to do with the mulled wine Mom's been refilling in everyone's glasses.

"So," Grandma says, dabbing her mouth with her napkin, "you two are staying until Monday morning, right?"

I nod, and Mom beams at that, even though I already told her beforehand. But now that she knows Garred and I are "dating," she's practically buzzing as she says, "It's great we won't have to bring the spare mattress from the garage. There's a queen-sized bed in Mitch's old room, so you'll be comfortable there."

It dawns on me what this means—Garred and I will be sleeping in one bed. I feel the blood rush from my face as I steal a quick glance at Garred, who's draped his hand over my chair and is nodding nonchalantly at my mom, like he doesn't have a care in the world.

This is the only thought buzzing in my head for the rest of dinner. After dessert, we exchange gifts, and after some more mulled wine, we start preparing for bed.

Once we're upstairs, my old room feels smaller than ever, probably because Garred takes up so much space in it. He's examining my old posters—Marvel movies, some indie bands, and, yes, the infamous *Twilight* poster that Mom never let me take down—while I'm frozen by the door, staring at the bed like it might bite.

"I can take the floor," Garred says suddenly, breaking the silence.

"What? No," I protest automatically, though my heart's racing. "You're too...tall for that." I almost say *big* but catch myself. "Your back would be killing you tomorrow."

He turns to face me, and in the soft glow of my bedside lamp, his expression is gentle. "Mitch, it's fine. I've slept in worse places during my shifts."

"No, really," I insist, trying to sound casual. "The bed's big enough. We're adults; we can handle sharing."

Garred raises an eyebrow, a hint of amusement on his lips. "Can we?"

I toss my toiletry bag at him, which he catches easily. "Shut up. Go brush your teeth."

While he's in the bathroom, I change into my pajamas at record speed—flannel pants and an old college T-shirt. I'm just finishing up when he comes back, fresh from his shower, still wearing my too-tight high school shirt. And briefs.

"Don't you want something more comfortable to sleep in?" I ask, trying not to stare at how the fabric clings to his chest.

"This is fine," he says, then grins. "Unless you're worried you won't be able to keep your hands to yourself?"

"You wish," I scoff, heading to the bathroom before he can see me blush, but I pause at the doorway. "And maybe ease up on the jokes, Garred. A more sensitive guy might've taken that last one as homophobic." I'm not actually offended—the smirk in my voice makes that clear—but I can't resist poking him for thinking he's so irresistible.

Garred looks genuinely puzzled. "How's that homophobic?" He lifts an eyebrow. "I'm literally flirting with you."

I freeze. Wait, what? My brain stalls, trying to process. Is this a joke? Because I'm too tired and tipsy to tell. Then again, maybe he's a bit tipsy too—his flushed cheeks seem to suggest it.

Garred gives me a sheepish smile. I blink, speechless, and quickly escape to the bathroom.

When I return, he's already in bed, lying on his back with one arm behind his head. He's taken off the shirt, and I nearly trip over my own feet. The moonlight streaming through the window highlights the lines of his chest, and I have to remind myself this is all pretend—that he's just playing a role and that I'm paying him for it. Well, sort of. With food.

"Your family's nice," he says as I awkwardly hover by the bed. "Even Adam, in his own way."

I snort and finally slide under the covers on my side. "Yeah, he's a real charmer."

"He cares about you," Garred says softly. "They all do. You can tell."

Something in his voice makes me turn my head. He's staring at the ceiling, his profile sharp in the moonlight.

"Yeah," I whisper. "I know."

"The way you described it, I pictured your family as really controlling, but they just seem a bit overprotective."

"They're on their best behavior because you're here," I scoff.

"Hm," he murmurs, but doesn't say anything more.

We lie there in silence for a minute, and I'm hyperaware of every inch of space between us. The bed suddenly feels both too big and too small at the same time.

"Thank you," I say finally. "For defending me at dinner. You didn't have to do that."

He turns his head to look at me, and our faces are closer than I expected. "Yes, I did."

My breath catches. "It's not...it's not part of what we agreed to."

"Maybe I just wanted to."

The air feels thick with possibility, and I have to look away. "Right. You're such a good actor, by the way."

Garred shifts beside me, and I feel his hand brush against mine under the covers. "Mitch..."

A knock at the door makes us both jump.

"Mitchell?" It's Mom. "I brought you boys some extra blankets. It gets cold up here at night."

I scramble out of bed and open the door, taking the blankets from her. She peers past me into the room, her eyes widening a bit at the sight of Garred's bare chest. I quickly say goodnight before she can start gushing again.

When I turn back around, Garred's watching me with an unreadable expression.

"What?" I ask, dropping the blankets at the foot of the bed.

"Nothing," he says, but he's smiling. "Just thinking about what a terrible liar you are."

"I am not!"

"You literally tripped over your words introducing me to your mom."

"Well, excuse me for not being a professional fake boyfriend like you," I grumble, sliding back into bed.

He laughs, the sound low and warm in the quiet room. "Trust me, I'm not as professional as you think."

I turn to face him, propping myself up on one elbow. "What's that supposed to mean?"

But Garred just smiles and closes his eyes. "Goodnight, Mitch."

I watch him for a moment longer, noticing the steady rise and fall of his chest, before lying back down. "Goodnight, Garred."

As I drift off to sleep, I swear I feel his fingers brush against mine under the covers. But maybe that's just my imagination—or the wine. Or maybe it's wishful thinking. Because this is all pretend, right?

...Right?

***

I wake to warmth.

Not just the usual bundled-under-blankets warmth, but a heat that seems to wrap around me completely. As I slowly come to my senses, I realize why: during the night, I somehow ended up pressed against Garred's chest, his arm draped heavily over my waist, our legs tangled beneath the sheets.

My first instinct is to pull away, but my body betrays me, wanting to sink deeper into his embrace. His chest rises and falls steadily against my back, his breath warm on my neck, and I'm struck by how natural this feels. Like we've done this a hundred times before.

I should move. I really should.

But then Garred shifts in his sleep, pulling me closer, his hand spreading across my stomach. My brain short-circuits as his fingers flex unconsciously, tracing gentle circles through the thin fabric of my T-shirt. I have to bite back a small gasp.

"Garred," I whisper, barely breathing.

"Mmhmm." His nose brushes the nape of my neck, his voice rough with sleep as he stirs but somehow pulls me even closer, sending a shiver down my spine.

"It's morning," I say, imagining the embarrassment he'll feel when he realizes it's me he's holding, not one of his firefighter groupies or something.

There's a pause, and I feel Garred tense slightly as he realizes our position. But he doesn't immediately pull away.

"Did you sleep okay?" he asks, his voice still low and gravelly. After a beat, he releases me, and I gain a little space between us, swallowing hard as I avoid his gaze.

"Yeah. You?"

"Like a baby," he says, and I can feel his smile. "Though someone's a bit of a blanket thief."

"I am not," I protest weakly, trying to ignore the lingering warmth of his touch on my skin.

"You absolutely are. At one point, I was freezing."

My heart stutters at his words. Is that what it was? Just sharing body heat?

The morning sun streams through my old curtains, painting stripes of gold across the bed, and somewhere outside, a bird starts singing.

Garred turns onto his side, watching me closely, noticing, maybe, how my thoughts are all over the place. I can't avoid looking at him any longer, and when I do, my breath catches.

His eyes are incredibly dark even in the morning light, flecked with gold, and they're fixed on mine with an intensity that makes my heart skip. His hair is tousled from sleep, curling slightly at the temples, and there's a hint of stubble along his jaw that definitely wasn't there yesterday. He looks... real. Human. Not the perfect fake boyfriend from last night, but someone tangible and flawed and beautiful.

"Mitch," Garred says softly, his voice serious now. "I should probably tell you something—"

But before he can continue, there's a knock at the door.

I can't believe my family's sense of comedic timing—just when Garred and I start to actually connect.

"Boys?" Mom calls out. "Breakfast in ten minutes! I'm making my special Christmas morning waffles!"

We almost spring apart like we've been shocked, and I nearly fall out of bed in my rush to put some distance between us. Garred catches my arm, steadying me, and the touch sends sparks up my skin.

"We'll be right down, Mrs. Collins!" Garred calls back, his voice remarkably steady despite the intensity in his eyes as he looks at me.

"Linda, dear! Remember?"

"Sorry—Linda!" he corrects, and we hear her happy footsteps heading back downstairs.

I look at Garred for a moment, noticing a slight flush on his cheeks that makes him look younger, somehow more vulnerable. The sheet has slipped to his waist, and I have to force myself to look away from the defined lines of his chest.

"What did you want to tell me?" I ask, biting my lip. I can feel that the moment has passed, but I still want to know.

Garred shakes his head. "Later, maybe."

"Yeah," I agree, gesturing vaguely toward the bathroom. "I'll take a quick shower."

"Yeah," he replies, running a hand through his hair.

I scoop up my clothes and practically flee to the bathroom, closing the door and leaning against it, heart pounding. What was all that? This whole morning? The memory of his touch lingers on my skin, and I end up splashing cold water on my face a few times before I can even think straight.

By the time I emerge, Garred's pulled on a fresh shirt—one of his own this time, thank god—and is making the bed with military precision. He looks up when I walk in, and something flickers in his eyes before he masks it with a casual smile.

"Bathroom's free," I say, fidgeting with the hem of my sweater.

He nods, grabbing his toiletry bag, but pauses as he passes me. For a moment, I think he's going to say whatever it was he wanted to say earlier—but instead, he reaches out and gently tucks a strand of my still-damp hair behind my ear.

"You look good in the morning," he says softly, then slips into the bathroom before I can respond.

I stand there, frozen, my ear tingling where his fingers brushed it, and wonder how I'm supposed to survive the entire day (and one more night) when I can barely handle breakfast.

Speaking of breakfast... I glance at the clock and realize we're already running late. Mom's Christmas morning waffles wait for no one—not even her son and his fake boyfriend.

***

The morning-after-Christmas waffles are a tradition as old as time itself, but today, I can barely taste them. Not with Garred's thigh pressed against mine under the table, not with him "accidentally" brushing his hand against mine as he reaches for the syrup, and definitely not when he lets out a low, appreciative moan after his first bite that nearly makes me choke on my coffee.

"These are incredible, Linda," he says, and Mom practically glows. "The hint of cinnamon is perfect."

"Finally, someone who appreciates my secret ingredient!" she beams, shooting me a look that clearly says, *keeper*.

I'm about to roll my eyes at her when Garred's fork appears in front of me, loaded with a piece of waffle dripping in maple syrup. "Try it with the strawberries," he says softly, holding a fresh berry in his other hand. "It's amazing."

Before I can think better of it, I lean forward and take the bite of strawberry, then the waffle from his fork. The mix of sweet and the slight sourness of the strawberry is delicious, but all I can focus on is the way Garred's eyes darken as he watches me. Or am I imagining things? I had so much mulled wine last night that I can't tell if I'm hallucinating.

A drop of syrup escapes the corner of my mouth, and Garred's thumb is there instantly, brushing it away and lingering on my bottom lip just a moment longer than necessary before he lifts it to his own mouth, licking it off his finger.

Someone clears their throat loudly, and we both jump. It's Adam, looking somewhere between amused and uncomfortable.

"Could you two maybe save it for after breakfast?" he asks dryly.

My face heats up, but Garred just grins, completely unapologetic. "Sorry," he says, not sounding sorry at all.

Claire giggles, elbowing Adam. "Oh, leave them alone. They're sweet."

"Too sweet," Adam mutters, though there's less bite in his tone than yesterday.

The morning sun streams through the kitchen windows, glinting off the remnants of syrup and melted butter on our plates. Steam rises from fresh cups of coffee as everyone settles into planning the day. There's something comforting about this moment—the way my family naturally falls into their rhythms, casually including Garred in their plans as if he's always been here.

"I'm taking these sugar monsters to see the holiday play at the community center," Rick says, trying to wrangle his youngest into a chair while she bounces in her Christmas pajamas. "'The Nutcracker' this year. Maybe it'll help burn off some of that candy cane energy."

Jemma dabs at a sticky spot on their daughter's chin, sharing a knowing look with her husband.

Mom adjusts her reading glasses, already making lists despite yesterday's feast. "Jemma and I need to get started on dinner soon. We've got all those lovely leftover sides, but I'm thinking of doing a honey-glazed ham tonight." She's in her element, her enthusiasm for feeding the family only heightened by yesterday's success.

"And I've got to take Claire to her check-up," Adam says over his second cup of coffee, his hand finding his wife's on the table. The gesture reminds me of how Garred held my hand earlier, and I have to look away.

Dad sips from the novelty mug I got him yesterday, the one covered in terrible dad jokes. "I'll be dropping your grandmother at her bridge club," he says, glancing up from his crossword. "Can't miss the post-Christmas tournament, can we, Mom?"

Grandma smirks, "Certainly not. The whole club's falling apart without proper leadership." She pats her cardigan pocket where her lucky cards are safely tucked. "Someone needs to restore order, and it might as well be me."

Through the comfortable chaos of clattering plates and overlapping conversations, Mom's voice cuts in with unusual enthusiasm. "What about you two?" She's looking at Garred and me with an expression I've never seen before—hopeful, almost glowing. "You should go explore the town! Everything's still decorated, and you could show Garred that little coffee shop you love. The one with the gingerbread lattes you used to go crazy for in high school."

I stare at her in disbelief. This is the same woman who had me peeling potatoes for three hours the day after Christmas last year, insisting she needed help with her famous post-Christmas dinner. But here she is, practically shooing us away from the house, beaming as she watches Garred snag another piece of bacon from my plate. He's been doing that since yesterday, treating my food like an extension of his own, and somehow I can't even pretend to be annoyed about it.

As the kitchen slowly empties, with everyone heading off to their errands and activities, I find myself alone with Mom, absently wiping down the already-clean counter. Garred's gone upstairs to change and take a shower, and I can hear the water running through the old pipes.

"You know," Mom says, carefully arranging the leftover waffles in a container, "I haven't seen you this happy in a long time."

I freeze mid-wipe. There's something in her voice, a softness that makes my chest ache. When I look up, her eyes are suspiciously bright.

"You're imagining things, Mom," I say, but she just waves me off with a dish towel.

"Let me say this," she insists, setting down the container. "I've been so worried about you, Mitchell. Not because you couldn't find someone, but because you never let anyone in." She takes a shaky breath. "I was afraid you'd end up alone, unhappy."

The guilt hits me like a physical blow, sharper than I expected. Here's my mother, practically glowing with joy because she thinks I've finally opened up to someone, and it's all built on a lie. The waffle I just ate sits like lead in my stomach. I tried to solve one problem, but it seems I've created another.

"We only just started dating," I say, trying to downplay it, knowing full well that on my next visit, Garred won't be with me.

"I know," Mom says. "But Garred," she continues, and my guilt doubles, "he sees you. Really sees you. The way he looks at you when you're distracted—like when you were telling that ridiculous story about your office Christmas party—it reminded me of your father in our early days."

I swallow hard, staring at the granite countertop as if it holds the secrets of the universe. "Mom, it's not—"

"And you know what else?" Mom leans in conspiratorially, dropping her voice to a stage whisper. "If you're worried he'll get bored, here's my advice: don't be passive in bed, dear."

I choke on air. "What?"

"It's important for a healthy relationship! Men need to feel desired, Mitchell. Even strong ones like Garred—especially strong ones. You have to show initiative—"

"Oh my god," I wheeze, wondering if it's possible to die

from second-hand embarrassment. The countertop suddenly seems like a great place to bang my head repeatedly.

A familiar laugh cuts through my mortification. Jemma's standing in the doorway, holding an empty coffee mug and looking like Christmas came twice this year.

"Mom," she says, barely containing her glee, "please stop traumatizing him. His face is matching the cranberry sauce."

"I'm trying to help!" Mom protests. "These things matter! Your father and I—"

"No!" I cut in desperately. "No dad stories. Please."

"All I'm saying is," Mom continues undeterred, "sometimes you need to take charge. Show him what you want. Be vocal about—"

"Don't listen to her, Mitch," Jemma interjects, mercifully. She sets her mug in the sink and gives me a knowing look. "The way Garred practically devours you with his eyes? Trust me, you're doing just fine."

I groan, slumping against the counter. "Can we please talk about literally anything else?"

"Now, when I was dating your father," Mom begins again, and I seriously consider making a break for the door, "I discovered that enthusiasm is key. It makes up for any lack of experience—"

"Mom!"

"—don't be afraid to experiment—"

"Please stop."

"—and remember, communication in the bedroom is crucial—"

"That's what I was telling him."

I whirl around so fast I nearly knock over the syrup bottle. Garred's standing in the doorway, hair damp from his shower, wearing that soft cream sweater that makes him look like he just stepped out of a winter fashion catalog. His expression is caught somewhere between amusement and something else I can't quite read.

"We need to go," I blurt out, already heading toward the door. "Right now. Immediately."

"But Mitchell, I haven't finished—"

"Bye, Mom, love you, see you later, thanks for breakfast!" I grab Garred's elbow and practically drag him toward the front door, Jemma's laughter echoing behind us.

In the hallway, I fumble with my coat zipper, my hands still shaking slightly from residual mortification. Garred gently moves my hands aside and zips it up for me, his fingers brushing against my chest.

"Your mom really knows what she's talking about," he says softly, a hint of teasing in his voice.

I look up at him and then roll my eyes. "Shut up," I mumble, trying to hide my embarrassment.

He holds my gaze a moment longer than necessary, then starts wrapping my scarf around my neck. "And," he says, his lips twitching, "I have to admit, I'm curious about those tips she was about to share—"

I shove him toward the door, my face burning. "Don't you dare."

His laugh follows us out into the crisp morning air, and as we crunch through the fresh snow, I try not to think about how natural it feels when he takes my hand. Or how my mom's happiness makes the lie feel heavier than ever. Or how, just maybe, Jemma might be right about the way Garred looks at me.

But mostly, I try not to think about how much I wish this wasn't pretend at all.

***

The frigid air hits us as we escape the house, and I silently thank whatever deity invented winter coats, because my face is burning so hot I might actually melt the snow around us. Garred keeps pace beside me, and I can feel him stealing glances, probably trying not to laugh at my mortification.

"So," he says after we've walked half a block in blessed silence.

"Don't." I hold up a warning finger. "We're never speaking of that conversation again."

A grin tugs at his lips. "Not even the part about—"

"Shush."

He laughs, the sound rich and warm in the crisp morning air. "Alright, baby. Lead the way."

My heart does a ridiculous little flip at the endearment, even though I know it's just part of our act. But there's no one around to act for, just empty, snow-covered sidewalks and the occasional car creeping carefully down the salted streets.

Around the corner, The Copper Bean appears, its brick facade dusted with snow.

"This is it," I say, pushing open the heavy wooden door. The warmth and familiar scent of coffee and cinnamon envelop us immediately. "My old teenage sanctuary. I still come here every time I'm home."

Not much has changed since my last visit over Thanksgiving—same exposed brick walls, worn wooden floors, and mismatched vintage furniture creating cozy nooks throughout the space. Holiday lights strung across the ceiling beams reflect off the copper accents that gave the place its name.

"The pastries smell amazing," Garred says, sniffing the air.

"I'm still stuffed from those waffles," I add as we join the short line, rubbing my stomach.

Garred smirks. "That's because you stole all the strawberries from my plate."

"Excuse me? You're the one who kept raiding *my* plate!"

His laugh draws the attention of the barista—Emma, with her ever-changing hair color, this month a pastel blue. She grins when she spots me.

"Hey, Mitch! Back for Christmas?" She glances at Garred with clear interest, then at how his hand rests casually on the small of my back. "And who's this?"

"Garred," he says, flashing his Hollywood smile. "Mitch's boyfriend."

Emma's eyebrows shoot up, and her grin widens. I can practically see her mentally composing a text to everyone in town—because in all my holiday visits home, I've never brought anyone with me.

"Just a gingerbread latte for me," I tell her quickly. "Still recovering from breakfast."

"Make that two gingerbread lattes," Garred says, then eyes the display case. "And one of those maple scones."

I raise an eyebrow. "How are you still hungry?"

He shrugs, an easy smile playing at his lips. "Firefighter metabolism." Then, quieter, just for me: "Besides, I'm sure you'll want some when you smell it."

God, why does it sound so filthy when he says it?

We find a corner table by a window overlooking the snowy street. Garred breaks off a piece of his scone and offers it to me without comment. When I shake my head, he offers it again, but I'm so full I can't even think about eating. So Garred pops both halves into his mouth, devours them in a second. A bit of pastry clings to his lower lip. Without thinking, I reach out to brush it away. The moment my fingers touch his skin, I freeze, realizing what I'm doing.

But Garred doesn't pull back. Instead, he catches my wrist gently, his thumb pressing against my pulse point. "Thanks," he says, his voice rougher than usual.

I withdraw my hand quickly, my skin tingling where he touched it. What am I doing? He's straight. Kelly said so, explicitly. This isn't real, no matter how real it feels when he looks at me like that.

"So," Garred says, mercifully breaking the moment, "is this where teenage Mitch plotted his escape from small-town life?"

I latch onto the change of subject, grateful for the distraction from my confusing thoughts. "Sort of. Though I mostly just read *Twilight* here and dodged my brother's attempts to drag me to football practice."

"Not a sports fan?"

"I'm not exactly into the whole getting-tackled-by-sweaty-men thing." I pause, realizing how that sounds, and feel my face heat up. "I mean—"

Garred cocks an eyebrow. "No judgment. Though as a firefighter, I can tell you sometimes getting tackled by sweaty men can save your life."

The way he says it, completely straight-faced but with that glint in his eyes—I can't tell if he's flirting or just teasing. That's the thing with Garred: everything he does seems to toe this maddening line between friendly and...something else.

"Point taken," I manage, taking a sip of my latte to hide my flustered expression. "Though I think getting tackled by you would be a bit more dangerous than getting tackled by high school football players."

Garred raises an eyebrow, a slow smile spreading across his face. "So you've thought this through, huh?"

I nearly choke on my coffee. "That's not—I meant because

you're—" I gesture vaguely at his everything, then realize that probably makes it worse.

"Because I'm what?" he asks innocently, though there's nothing innocent about the way he's looking at me.

Before I can dig myself into an even deeper hole, my phone buzzes. It's a text from Kelly.

Kelly: How's it going with your straight prince charming? ●

The reminder hits like a bucket of cold water. Right. Straight. I quickly type back.

Mitch: Fine. Everything's fine.

When I look up, Garred's watching me with an unreadable expression. "Kelly checking up on us?" So he looked at my screen to see who was messaging me.

"Yeah," I say, pocketing my phone. "Making sure you haven't run screaming from my family yet."

"No chance of that." He leans forward, his knee bumping against mine under the table. "I'm actually having fun playing boyfriend. You're easier to date than I expected."

Something in my chest twists. *Playing boyfriend.* "What did you expect?"

"I don't know." His fingers trace the rim of his cup. "Kelly talks about you all the time, but she never mentioned how easy you are to talk to or be around. Or how cute you get when you're flustered."

I feel my face heat up again. "I'm not—"

"Like *that*," he says softly. "Exactly like that."

At that moment, Emma swings by with fresh coffee. "Refill?" she asks, but her eyes are darting between us with obvious interest.

"No, thanks," Garred says, still looking at me. "We're already leaving." He stands in one smooth motion, extending his hand to me. Without thinking, I take it, his palm warm against mine.

He doesn't let go, even after we step outside into the sharp winter air.

"Want to go home already?" I ask, still a bit dazed by our earlier conversation.

He gives me a sidelong glance that makes my stomach flip. "No. I want you to show me around while the light's good."

***

The winter air feels sharp after the coffee shop's warmth, but Garred keeps hold of my hand as we walk, his thumb absently stroking my knuckles. The gesture seems unconscious, like he doesn't even realize he's doing it, which somehow makes it worse.

Main Street stretches before us, strung with holiday lights that haven't been turned on yet, though the winter afternoon is already fading into dusk. The cold has kept most people inside, giving the snow-covered sidewalks an intimate feel, like we're walking through our own private snow globe.

"This place doesn't really change," I say, watching our breath mist in the cold air. "Every Christmas, same decorations, same shops, same everything."

"And you come back every year?"

"Yeah. Actually, a couple of times a year." I pause. "Sometimes I think about visiting more, but..." I trail off, distracted by the way his thumb is drawing small circles on my palm.

"But?"

I glance up at him, caught off guard by the genuine interest in his voice. "It's complicated. Coming home always feels like stepping back in time. Like everyone's waiting to see if I've finally become the person they expected me to be."

Garred's hand tightens around mine. "And who's that?"

"I don't know. Someone more like Adam, maybe. Successful, settled, pursuing the whole American dream thing." I laugh, but it comes out a bit hollow. "Instead, they got me—still assistant editing other people's stories instead of writing my own, still single, still..." I trail off, suddenly aware I'm revealing way too much.

"Still perfectly fine exactly as you are," Garred says quietly, pulling me closer as we pass a patch of ice. His arm slides around my waist, steadying me, though I'm pretty sure I didn't actually stumble.

We pass the old cinema, its art deco facade gleaming with fresh snow. The marquee advertises IT'S A WONDERFUL LIFE—*Christmas Eve showing!*

"They do this every year," I tell him, grateful for the distraction from how natural it feels to be tucked against his side. "Half the town shows up. Everyone knows all the lines, but they still cry at the end."

"Did you used to come here?" Garred asks, nodding toward the cinema. "To watch movies with Kelly?"

"Yeah," I laugh, remembering those awkward teenage years. "She'd drag me to every single romance movie. Said I needed to learn how to be boyfriend material." I pause, suddenly self-conscious. "Guess she was right."

Garred pulls me closer, his warmth radiating through his winter coat. "I don't know. You seem like perfect boyfriend material to me."

My heart skips a beat. "Says the guy who's literally *paid* to pretend I'm his boyfriend."

"Paid *with food*," he corrects, his voice soft. "And honestly, you're making it pretty easy."

Before I can process that, a snowflake lands on my nose. Then another. And another. Soon, fat, lazy flakes are drifting down around us, catching in Garred's dark hair and settling on his eyelashes. He looks like something out of a Christmas card or a Hallmark movie, and I have to remind myself to breathe.

"Come on," he says, tugging my hand. "I want to see more."

We walk past the old bookstore where I spent countless summer afternoons, the vintage record shop that still has the same faded posters in the window, the ice cream parlor that somehow stays open year-round. At each spot, Garred asks questions—genuine ones, like he really wants to know about my life here, about the person I used to be.

"This is where I came out to Kelly," I say as we pass the small park with its frozen fountain. "She hugged me so hard I thought my ribs would crack. Then she made me promise to tell her about every guy I ever dated." I smile at the memory. "It was zero then. She's still waiting for that list to get longer than two names."

Garred's quiet for a moment, his thumb still tracing patterns on my palm. "Only two?"

"Yeah," I admit, watching a cardinal land on a snow-covered branch. "I'm not great at...this. The whole relationship thing."

"I'm not either," Garred says, though it sounds almost too modest, considering he practically charmed my whole family in a day.

"Are you joking? You're ridiculously good at this," I tell him, mock-offended. "If I didn't know you were a firefighter, I'd think you did this for a living. The fake boyfriend thing. You're gorgeous, you have the charm, the manners, the brains...you're like a total package." I blurt it out before I can stop myself, and Garred actually blushes.

"God, Mitch..." He laughs softly.

Something in his voice makes me look up. He's already watching me, snowflakes melting on his cheeks, and his expression makes my breath catch. Before I can stop myself,

I reach up to brush some snow from his hair. His eyes darken, and he catches my wrist, holding my hand against his cheek.

"Mitch," he breathes, and just the way he says my name makes my heart pound. He leans in, our faces just inches apart.

I don't know who moves first—maybe we both do. One moment we're standing in the snow, and the next his lips brush against mine, so softly it's barely a touch. It's tender, almost like he's asking permission. His breath mingles with mine, warm in the cold air, and then he kisses me again, more certain this time.

His lips are impossibly soft against mine, and I feel myself melting under his touch like snow in sunlight. One of his hands comes up to cup my face, his thumb stroking my cheek with such tenderness it makes my heart ache. The other hand rests on my sweater beneath my open coat, steady and warm. I reach up hesitantly, fingers finding the soft wool of his sweater, and he smiles against my lips.

The kiss stays slow and sweet, exploring. His lips move against mine with careful precision, like he's mapping every detail, committing it to memory. When I sigh into his mouth, his grip on my waist tightens slightly. The hand on my cheek slides into my hair, cradling the back of my head as he tilts my face, deepening the kiss with a thoroughness that's almost devastating.

Then something shifts. Maybe it's the way I cling to his sweater or the small sound I make when his tongue grazes my bottom lip—but suddenly, the kiss transforms from tender to hungry. His tongue slides against mine, and the taste of him— coffee, sweetness, and something uniquely Garred—makes me dizzy with want.

He kisses me like he's drowning and I'm air, like he's been starving for this. His hand fists in my hair, not rough but insistent, holding me exactly where he wants me as he explores my mouth. His other arm wraps fully around my waist, pulling me close until I feel the heat of his body through our winter layers. I arch into him instinctively, and he makes this low sound in his throat that sends shivers down my spine.

I lose myself in it completely—in the way his tongue slides against mine, in the little bites he places on my lower lip, in the way he soothes each one with a sweep of his tongue. My hands move of their own accord, one sliding up to his neck to feel his pulse racing under my fingers, the other gripping his shoulder for balance as my knees go embarrassingly weak.

He kisses me deeper, harder, like he's trying to consume me. Then he gentles it again, slow and thorough, taking his time to taste every corner of my mouth. When I whimper—actually whimper—he groans softly and pulls me closer, one hand sliding up my back to hold me tight as his tongue does wicked, wonderful things that make me forget we're standing in the middle of a snowy street.

I'm lost in a haze of sensation—the heat of his mouth, the strength of his hands, the solid warmth of his body against mine. He tastes like winter and promises, and I want to drown in him. Everything narrows down to this: his lips on mine, his hands holding me like I'm precious, the desperate little sounds he makes when I kiss him back...

"Well, well, well."

Adam's voice shatters the moment like thin ice cracking. We break apart, but not completely—Garred keeps his arm around my waist, and I'm grateful for it because I'm not entirely sure my legs will hold me up.

I turn around. Adam and Claire are standing a few feet away, and oh god, they just watched me practically devour my fake boyfriend in the middle of Main Street. Claire looks delighted, but Adam's expression is unreadable.

My lips feel swollen, tingling from the kiss, and I can still taste Garred on my tongue. When I dare to look at him, his pupils are blown wide, his cheeks flushed, and there's something wild and hungry in his eyes that makes my breath catch.

"Sorry to interrupt," Claire says, not sounding sorry at all.

And just like that, the spell breaks completely. Of course—Garred saw them coming. He must have. This was all for show, another perfect performance from my fake boyfriend. The warmth of his kiss turns to ice in my chest as I realize that none of it was real.

Was it?

"All good with the check-up?" Garred asks casually, like he hasn't just kissed me senseless, like my whole world hasn't just tilted on its axis.

"Perfect!" Claire beams, rubbing her belly. "The little one's growing right on schedule."

I barely hear their conversation. My mind races, replaying every second of that kiss. The tenderness, the hunger, the way he held me like...but no. No. It was all an act. A brilliant performance for my brother's benefit. Garred probably saw them coming and seized the opportunity to make our relationship look more convincing. That's why he kissed me so thoroughly, why he made it look so real.

Because he's good at this. Too good.

"Mitch?" Claire's voice cuts through my spiral. "You okay? You look a bit pale."

"Just cold," I lie, wrapping my arms around myself and stepping slightly away from Garred. I can't handle his touch right now—not when I'm still tingling from his kiss, not when every part of me wants to believe it meant something.

"Let's get some hot chocolate," Claire suggests, but I shake my head.

"Actually, we should head back," I say quickly. "Mom's probably waiting on us for dinner prep, and you know how she gets."

"True," Adam agrees, checking his watch. "It's almost time for dinner anyway."

The walk back is torture. Claire happily chatters about the baby, with Adam occasionally chiming in, while Garred responds with all the right words at all the right moments. I can feel his eyes on me, sense him trying to catch my gaze, but I keep my eyes fixed firmly on the snowy sidewalk.

When we reach the house, the warmth and smell of Mom's cooking wrap around us, but even the comfort of home can't calm the chaos in my chest.

"There you are!" Mom calls from the kitchen as soon as we're free of our coats and boots. "I was starting to worry. Mitch, honey, can you help me with the potatoes? Garred, dear, would you mind helping Jemma set the table?"

"Of course," Garred says smoothly, but he catches my arm before I can slip away to the kitchen. "Mitch, can we—"

"Later," I cut him off, pulling away. "Mom's waiting."

In the kitchen, I throw myself into peeling and slicing with desperate energy, trying to drown out my thoughts in the rhythm of cooking. But every time I close my eyes, I feel his lips on mine again, taste the coffee and sweetness on his tongue, feel the strength of his hands...

"Mitch, honey," Mom says suddenly, making me jump. "You're massacring those boiled potatoes. I need them sliced for frying."

I look down at the mangled mess I've made of what should have been elegant slices. "Sorry," I mutter.

Mom wipes her hands on her apron, giving me that look—the one that says she sees right through me. "Did something happen with you and Garred?"

"No," I say too quickly. "Everything's fine."

"Mmhmm." She doesn't sound convinced. "That's why you're standing in my kitchen trying to turn perfectly good potatoes into mash while looking like someone kicked your cat?"

"Mom..."

"You know," she says carefully, "when your father and I first started dating—"

"Please," I interrupt, "no more relationship stories. I can't...I just can't right now."

She studies me for a long moment, then sighs. "Alright. But Mitch? Whatever's going on in that overthinking head of yours? Maybe try talking to him about it instead of taking it out on my veggies."

Before I can respond, Garred appears in the doorway. "Table's set," he says softly. "Need any help in here?"

"Perfect timing!" Mom beams. "You can help Mitch fry these potatoes in that garlic-infused oil while I go call Dad. He should've been back with Grandma by now."

Then she's gone, leaving us alone in the kitchen. The silence between us feels heavy and tense as we work, frying the potatoes and avoiding each other's gaze. Minutes pass, each one stretching out longer than the last.

"Mitch," Garred finally says, stepping a little closer. "About earlier—"

"You don't have to explain," I say, keeping my eyes on the potatoes. "I get it."

"I really don't think you do."

"Adam was there, and you had to make it look convincing," I say. "You did great. Really sold it."

"That's what you think?" His voice is strange, almost hurt. "That I kissed you because Adam was watching?"

Finally, I look up at him, meeting his gaze. "Didn't you?"

"No," Garred says roughly. And before I can process it, he's crowding me against the counter, his hands gripping my waist. "I kissed you because I've been wanting to since Halloween."

Then his mouth is on mine, crashing into me, and this kiss is nothing like the one on the street. There's no gentleness now, no careful exploration—just heat and hunger from the first touch. His tongue pushes into my mouth, demanding and possessive, and I can't hold back the moan that escapes me.

His hands slide down my back, settling lower, gripping my ass as he presses me harder against the counter. The edge digs into my hips, but I barely register it because Garred is everywhere—the solid heat of his chest against me, the insistent sweep of his tongue in my mouth, the low growl he makes when I dig my fingers into his hair and pull him even closer.

One of his hands slips up under my sweater, his palm searing against my skin, and I arch into his touch shamelessly. He uses the movement to slide one thick thigh between my legs, pressing up in a way that makes me gasp into his mouth. His other hand cups the back of my neck, tilting my head just so as he deepens the kiss like he's trying to devour me whole.

"God, Mitch," he breathes against my lips before moving down to my neck. His teeth graze my pulse point, and my knees nearly buckle. But he's got me pinned so thoroughly against the counter that I couldn't fall even if I tried. His mouth is hot and hungry on my throat, alternating between kisses and sharp little bites that send sparks of pleasure down my spine.

I'm making these embarrassing little whimpering sounds, but I can't help it—not when he's sucking what will definitely be a mark into my neck, not when his hands roam possessively over my body like he owns me, not when his thigh is still pressed exactly where I need it. My hips roll forward instinctively, seeking friction, and the sound he makes against my throat is almost feral. Thankfully, there's music playing in the dining room, loud enough to cover any sounds we're making, a small mercy as I lose myself completely in him.

"Wanted this," Garred pants between kisses, "wanted you—"

The front door opens with a loud thud, and we spring apart like we've been electrocuted. I stumble slightly, grabbing the counter for support as Garred takes a few quick steps back. We're both breathing hard, and I know I must look absolutely wrecked—lips swollen, hair tousled from his hands, probably with a spectacular hickey on my neck.

Mom's footsteps echo in the hallway as she walks past the kitchen door, calling out, "Dad and Grandma are back! Dinner in ten minutes!"

I don't dare look at Garred as I adjust my sweater with trembling hands. My whole body is thrumming, my skin still burning everywhere he touched. The kitchen feels too small, too hot, charged with everything left unsaid.

My thoughts race like galloping horses. I have so many questions, but I know now isn't the time—not with my family in the next room. So we finish frying the potatoes in silence, though I can still feel my heart pounding, feel the electricity sparking between us. When Garred's hand brushes mine as I pass him the serving dish, I nearly drop it.

Just before we head to the dining room, Garred catches my wrist, his lips inches from my ear. "Mitch," he says, his voice still rough enough to send a shiver down my spine, "God, I want you." I take in his disheveled hair, dark eyes, the flush high on his cheeks.

His words make my heart flip, and I'm practically radiating heat. He nips at my earlobe, sucking it gently into his mouth, and my knees nearly buckle. I feel dizzy, like I'm barely holding myself together.

Oh. My. God.

As we step out into the dining room, my heart is still hammering, and I can barely think straight. Because maybe—just maybe—this isn't as fake as I thought.

Chapter 5
The Truth

Dinner is excruciating.

I can barely focus on anything happening around me, hyperaware of Garred's every movement beside me. His thigh keeps pressing against mine under the table, and every time he reaches for something, his arm brushes my shoulder. The spot where he kissed my neck throbs gently, and I'm grateful for the high collar of my sweater.

Mom keeps the conversation flowing, but I barely register what anyone's saying. All I can think about is the kitchen, the way Garred kissed me, the things he whispered. My hands shake slightly as I cut my food, and when Garred passes me the salt, our fingers brush, sending electricity up my arm.

"Mitchell?" Grandma's voice breaks through my haze. "Did you hear what I asked?"

"Sorry, what?" I blink, realizing everyone's looking at me.

"I was asking if you boys enjoyed your walk around town," she says, her eyes twinkling knowingly.

I feel my face heat up. "Oh. Yeah, it was...nice."

"Very nice," Garred adds, his voice low and warm.

"Right," Adam says meaningfully, faint annoyance lacing his words.

After what feels like hours, dinner finally winds down. As everyone starts clearing the table, Garred catches my eye and tilts his head slightly toward the stairs. The gesture is subtle, but it sends my heart racing. I manage a small nod, trying to look casual as we slip away from the cleanup chaos.

We barely make it through my bedroom door before Garred's on me, backing me against the wall, his mouth crashing into mine with a desperation that makes me dizzy. For a moment, I lose myself in it—in the heat of his lips, in the way his hands grip my hips, in the soft groan he makes when I arch against him. But then reality crashes back in, and I pull away, pressing my palms against his chest.

"Wait," I breathe, my voice shaky. "Are you...? Kelly said you were straight."

Garred pulls back just enough to look at me, his eyes dark with desire but clouded with confusion. "She said what?"

"She told me explicitly that you were 'straight as an arrow.'" Even now, I can hear her voice saying those words, remember how my heart sank when she said them.

He lets out a surprised laugh, his breath warm against my lips. "What? No. I'm very much gay. I told her that last week when she tried to seduce me after one of your bar nights." His hands haven't left my waist, his thumbs drawing maddening circles through my sweater. "Actually, that night, I told her I had a crush on you."

"Oh God," I mumble, my mind racing. "Why wouldn't she tell me?"

Garred frowns, and I can practically see his thoughts aligning with mine. I know Kelly—know how her mind works. She must have been mortified about coming onto Garred only to find out he was gay. But that doesn't explain why she kept his feelings for me a secret.

And then it hits me. "She set this whole thing up."

"What?" Garred's brows furrow adorably.

"That's why she looked so pleased with herself when she came up with this fake boyfriend thing." The pieces are falling into place. "But she probably knew I'd spoil everything if I knew you were gay. Or that you had feelings for me." I shake my head, a mix of exasperation and fondness washing over me. "She knows what an overthinker I am."

A slow smirk spreads across Garred's face. "That's a little twisted," he says, "but knowing Kelly? I can absolutely see her doing that." He laughs softly, then pulls me closer, his lips brushing the shell of my ear. "Mitch, I've been in love with you since that night you spent twenty minutes explaining why vampires would definitely beat firefighters."

A laugh bubbles out of me, nervous and warm, my heart feeling like it might burst. "That long?"

He nods, pressing his forehead against mine. "That long. And then Kelly came up with this ridiculous plan, and I thought maybe..." He takes a shaky breath, and I feel it against my lips. "Maybe if I could show you how good we could be together, you'd want this to be real. Want me." His eyes darken as they search mine.

"I—" My voice catches as his hands tighten on my waist. "I want you. Have wanted you. But I thought you were straight."

"Don't you know that all firefighters are gay?" Garred smirks, referencing Adam's idiotic comment from last night, and I can't help but laugh again.

Then his mouth is on mine again, but this time, there's no hesitation, no doubt—just heat and want and the pure joy of knowing this is real. His hands thread through my hair as he walks me backward toward the bed, and I know we should probably go back downstairs before someone comes looking for us, but right now, all I can think about is how perfectly we fit together, how right this feels.

The pretending is over. This is real.

The back of my knees hit the mattress, and Garred follows me down as I fall, bracing himself above me. His weight pins me deliciously against the bed, and when he kisses me again, it's deep and thorough, like he's trying to make up for all the time we've lost pretending.

"God, you're beautiful," he murmurs against my lips, and I flush all the way down my neck. His mouth follows the blush, trailing hot kisses down my throat, lingering on the mark he left earlier. When he bites down gently, I have to bite my lip to stifle a moan.

"Shh," he whispers, but I can feel him smirking against my skin. "Don't want the whole family to hear."

"Then stop doing that with your—oh!" I gasp as his teeth graze a particularly sensitive spot. His laugh rumbles against my neck, and I tug his hair in retaliation, which only makes him groan and press me harder into the mattress.

His hands slip under my sweater, palms hot against my skin as they slide up my sides. I arch into his touch, forgetting to be quiet, and a rather embarrassing whimper escapes me when his thumbs brush over my nipples.

"Baby," he breathes, pulling back to look at me with dark eyes. "You have to be quieter than that."

"Make me," I challenge, and his eyes flash dangerously before he captures my mouth in a kiss that steals my breath. His tongue slides against mine, deep and possessive, while his hands continue their maddening exploration under my sweater.

I try to stay quiet, but it's nearly impossible. When his thigh presses between my legs, I moan into his mouth, and he has to swallow the sound with another searing kiss. My hands roam over his back, feeling the play of muscles under his sweater and undershirt, and when I scratch lightly down his spine, he makes this broken sound that goes straight to my core.

"Fuck, Mitch," he pants against my mouth. "Do you have any idea how long I've wanted this?"

I pull him down for another kiss, hooking one leg around his waist to bring him closer. The friction makes us both gasp, and Garred breaks away to press his forehead against mine, breathing hard.

"If you keep doing that," he warns, voice rough, "I'm not going to last very long."

The sound of voices drifting up from downstairs breaks through our heated moment.

"Has anyone seen my keys?" Jemma calls out.

"Check under the gift wrapping!" Mom responds.

We both freeze, then share a look that's equal parts frustrated and amused. "We should probably..." I gesture vaguely toward the door.

"Yeah," Garred agrees reluctantly, pressing one last kiss to my lips before rolling off me. We take a moment to straighten our clothes and try to look less... thoroughly kissed. I catch a glimpse of us in my old mirror—flushed cheeks, mussed hair, swollen lips—and have to bite back a laugh.

Downstairs, we find everyone gathering their coats and gifts. Jemma catches my eye across the hallway as she's helping her youngest into her coat. Once the kids are bundled up, she makes her way over to us, that knowing smile playing on her lips.

"You know," she says, studying us both with that big-sister

intensity, "I've never seen you like this before, Mitch." There's something gentle in her voice, a warmth that makes me squirm a little.

"Jem—" I start, but she pulls me into a tight hug.

"I'm so happy for you, little brother," she whispers, and there's something in her voice that makes my throat tight. When she pulls back, her eyes are suspiciously bright.

Then she turns to Garred, and I expect her usual protective sister routine. Instead, she hugs him, too, which seems to surprise him as much as it does me. "Welcome to the family, officially," she says warmly. "And thank you for making him smile like that. I haven't seen him this happy since...well, maybe ever."

Adam approaches next, hands stuffed in his pockets, looking characteristically uncomfortable with emotional moments. He clears his throat. "So."

"So," I reply, tensing slightly.

He shifts his weight, glancing between Garred and me, then focuses on adjusting his coat zipper. "You know how I get sometimes," he says gruffly. Coming from Adam, it's practically a declaration of remorse. "Being the older brother and all."

"Yeah," I say, understanding what he's not saying. With Adam, it's always about what's not said.

He nods once, then turns to Garred. For a moment, they just look at each other, doing that weird masculine assessment thing. Then Adam extends his hand. "Take care of him," he says simply. It's not quite a threat, not quite a blessing, but something in between.

"I will," Garred replies with equal gravity, and I roll my eyes at their dramatics, even as something warm blooms in my chest.

Then Grandma practically bounces over to us, her eyes

twinkling with barely contained glee. She wraps her arms around both of us at once, pulling us down to her level with surprising strength.

"Oh, my boys!" she exclaims, patting both our cheeks. "Finally, someone worthy of my Mitchell!" She beams up at Garred. "You make sure he has some proper fun, dear. Though," she adds with a decidedly wicked wink that makes me want to melt into the floor, "judging by that mark on his neck, you're already doing a fine job."

"Grandma!" I choke out, mortified, as Garred tries and fails to suppress his laugh.

The rest of the goodbyes are a blur of hugs and kisses. Jemma and Rick wrangle their sleepy kids toward the door while Claire gives us one last warm smile. Dad helps Grandma with her coat, and then they're all filing out into the snowy night, car doors slamming and engines starting up one by one.

As the last taillights disappear down the street, we're left standing in the warm light of the entryway with Mom. Then, suddenly, Mom starts gathering her things with an air of studied nonchalance that immediately sets off warning bells in my head. She adjusts her reading glasses, checks her phone, and casually reaches for her coat, all with an overdone calmness that screams she's up to something. I watch her, suspicion growing as she pretends to be deeply interested in her scarf's alignment.

"Well," she says, smoothing it down, "I should probably get going."

I blink at her. "Going? Where?"

"Mhmm," she hums, buttoning up her coat with deliberate care. "Samantha's expecting me for our movie night. Your father will join us after he drops off Grandma."

I stare at her, confused. Mom has never just…left when I

was here. She's usually the one insisting I stay longer, always finding an excuse to keep me around—pulling out old photo albums or saying there's "just one more thing" to show me. Her sudden departure feels strange, and I can't shake the feeling that there's more to it than meets the eye.

"I'll be gone for a few hours at least," she interrupts, a little too cheerfully. "Probably won't be back until quite late, actually."

Something about her tone makes me suspicious, but I can't quite put my finger on why until she adds, far too casually, "Oh, and Mitchell? The first aid kit in the upstairs bathroom has a new pack of condoms in it. Just in case you boys need anything."

Oh. Oh, god. OH, GOD.

My face blazes so hot I'm surprised I don't burst into flames. Beside me, Garred makes a strangled sound that might be a laugh or a cough.

"Mom!" I manage to croak out, but she's already heading for the door, keys jingling in her hand.

"Don't wait up!" she calls over her shoulder, and then she's gone, leaving me standing there in mortified silence while Garred shakes with silent laughter next to me.

"I can't believe she just—" I start, then cover my face with my hands. "Oh god, this is so embarrassing."

"I don't know," Garred says, his voice warm with amusement as he pulls me closer. "I think it's kind of sweet. In a thoroughly mortifying way."

"Sweet?" I wince, almost painfully. "My mother just cleared out the house so we could have sex!"

Garred must sense my panic because his expression softens as he pulls me into his arms. "Hey," he says, his voice gentle. "No pressure. We don't have to do anything."

I let out a shaky laugh against his chest. "I feel like there's a spreadsheet somewhere with designated positions and performance metrics. Probably with a satisfaction survey at the end."

His laugh rumbles through his chest, and I feel some of the tension ease from my shoulders. "From what I've learned about your mom in the last twenty-four hours," he chuckles, "I wouldn't be surprised if she's already planning our wedding." His hands stroke soothingly up and down my arms. "But seriously, Mitch. We can just...go to sleep."

I pull back slightly to look at him, struck again by how unfairly gorgeous he is in the soft hallway light. "Wine?" I suggest, my voice only slightly unsteady. "We still have that other bottle from yesterday."

"Lead the way," he says, pressing a quick kiss to my temple that somehow makes me more nervous than all our heated kisses upstairs.

In the kitchen, I fumble with the corkscrew while Garred leans against the counter, watching me with those dark eyes that seem to see right through me. The air feels thick with possibility, charged with everything we've said and everything we haven't.

"Need help with that?" he asks, amusement coloring his voice as I struggle with the cork. "We don't want a repeat of yesterday's wine incident, do we?"

"I got it," I insist, though my hands are trembling slightly. After another moment of wrestling, the cork finally pops free. "And I don't know," I say, trying for lightness despite my racing heart. "You looked pretty good in my tiny T-shirt."

Garred's eyes darken at that, and he steps closer, crowding me against the counter in a way that's becoming wonderfully familiar. "Yeah?" he says softly. "Is that why you were staring?"

"I wasn't—" I start to protest, but he just raises an eyebrow, and I feel my face heat up. "Okay, maybe I was staring a little."

He laughs, the sound low and warm, then reaches past me to grab two wine glasses from the cabinet. His chest brushes against mine, and I catch the faint scent of his cologne—pine, and spice, and something uniquely him. The casual intimacy of the moment makes my heart race, and suddenly, I can't ignore the nervous energy thrumming through me.

Now that I know this is real—that Garred is actually gay, actually wants me—the stakes feel impossibly high. It's not just about tonight anymore. Every touch, every look carries the weight of possibility and god, I don't want to mess this up.

All those times I'd seen him at his and Kelly's apartment, I'd forced myself not to stare too long, convinced myself not to read into his friendly smiles. Someone like him was so far out of my league that I hadn't even let myself imagine the possibility. But now he's here, so close, and I'm terrified of doing something wrong.

"We should..." I gesture vaguely toward the stairs with my wine glass, my voice slightly unsteady. "Maybe go up?"

Garred nods, his eyes never leaving mine as he follows me up the stairs. The walk feels endless, and I'm buzzing with anticipation. When we reach the second floor, I hesitate outside my bedroom door, suddenly unsure.

"So," I start, then take a large gulp of wine for courage. "Is this like...a one-time thing? Or...?"

The words come out in a rush, and I immediately want to kick myself. But Garred's expression shifts from amused to intense so quickly it steals my breath.

"No," he says roughly, stepping closer until I feel his hot breath on my face. His free hand comes up to cup my jaw, thumb brushing my lower lip. "God, no."

The conviction in his voice sends butterflies racing through my chest. He sets his wine glass on the hallway table without looking, then takes mine and sets it aside, too. When he turns back to me, his eyes are obsidian with want.

"I want all of it," he says, voice low and serious, "The boyfriend stuff. The family stuff. I plan to take my time with you. To learn every inch of you." His hands slide down to my hips, pulling me flush against him. "To figure out exactly what makes you fall apart." He punctuates this by pressing a hot, open-mouthed kiss to my neck. "And then do it again and again until you can't remember your own name."

I let out an embarrassing whimper that seems to spur him on. His mouth finds mine in a kiss that's all tongue, wet heat, and promise, and my knees actually buckle. He catches me easily, one strong arm around my waist, and I can barely catch my breath with how much I want him.

Then suddenly, he pulls back, eyes dancing with mischief even as his chest heaves. "So," he says, voice rough but playful, "Kelly mentioned you read those spicy romantasy novels. How am I doing? Living up to your book boyfriend expectations?"

I laugh breathlessly, grateful for the moment of levity even as my heart races. "Did she tell you everything about me?"

"Only the embarrassing bits," he murmurs with a chuckle, pressing a softer kiss to my lips. "Though I have to say, I'm a little jealous of all those brooding immortal warriors you spend your nights with."

"Shut up," I manage, though I can't help smiling. His answering grin is wicked as he nudges my nose with his.

"You know," he says thoughtfully, voice low and teasing, "I may not be immortal, but I bet I can make you squirm just as much." His hands slide down to cup me through my jeans, and I curse under my breath at the touch.

The playfulness in his voice does nothing to hide the heat in his eyes, and whatever clever response I might have had dies in my throat as he leans in to trace his tongue along my jaw. Every touch feels electric, heightened by the knowledge that this is real, that he actually wants this—wants me.

"Yes," I gasp as his tongue finds the column of my throat. "We should—the bedroom."

He pulls back just enough to look at me, his eyes dark and intense. "You sure?"

The genuine care in his voice, even now, makes my heart flip. I nod, not trusting my voice, and reach for the doorknob behind me.

The door clicks open, and we stumble through it, not wanting to break contact. Garred kicks it shut behind us, and for a moment, we just look at each other in the soft moonlight filtering through my old curtains.

His kisses are gentle at first, almost reverent, but they quickly deepen as I press closer, wanting more. His hands slide under my sweater, leaving trails of fire across my skin, and I arch into his touch.

"Can I...?" he asks, fingers touching the hem of my sweater. I nod, raising my arms so he can pull it off. The cool air hits my skin, and then he drops to his knees, his mouth finding my chest, leaving warm, wet kisses down to my stomach. "Fuck," he breathes against my skin before standing and backing me toward the bed.

My knees hit the mattress, and I pull him down with me. His sweater feels rough against my bare chest, and I tug at it impatiently until he sits up, pulling off both it and his undershirt. The sight of him above me in the moonlight takes my breath away. He's looking at me with such intensity, such desire that I feel my heart might burst. This isn't pretend anymore—this is real, this is us finally being honest about what we want.

Garred leans down to kiss me again, his tongue sliding against mine as his hands explore my bare chest. His weight pins me to the mattress in the most delicious way, and I can't help but moan and arch up against him, seeking more contact.

"Fuck, Mitch," he breathes against my neck, alternating between kisses and gentle bites. "The sounds you make..."

I would be embarrassed by the whimpers escaping me, but I'm too lost in sensation—the heat of his mouth, the strength of his hands, the way he keeps grinding against me like he can't help himself.

His touch drives me crazy, and I reach for his belt buckle, needing more. He helps me ease his jeans off before slipping mine down, too, and soon we're both down to just our underwear, skin burning everywhere we connect. I slide his briefs down, and for a moment, I'm completely at a loss—my mind struggling to keep up with the sight of him, both vulnerable and confident, his cock so big and aroused it makes my head spin.

He slides my boxers off, and the sound he makes when he sees me naked and aroused is almost feral. His kiss grows demanding, possessive, as his hands grip my hips. Instinctively, my legs wrap around his waist, pulling him closer, and as he rocks against me, the friction makes us both groan in unison.

"Fuck, Mitch," he pants against my mouth, his hips rolling forward, sending stars through my vision as his cock presses hard against mine.

"We might...need a condom," I murmur, breathless.

"Yes," he gasps between kisses, but before I can move, his hand wraps around me, drawing a moan I can't hold back. He strokes me up and down, his thumb teasing over the sensitive head with each pass.

"Fuck," I gasp as Garred quickens his pace, his rough palm igniting every nerve, each stroke sending heat rippling through me. Just as I feel myself teetering on the edge, he pauses, spits on his hand, and then resumes, his grip firmer, making me shiver from head to toe. The pleasure coils tighter, building in waves, but I'm not ready to let go. Leaning close, I whisper against his ear, my voice breathless, "Fuck me."

His hand freezes mid-stroke, and his eyes darken with unmistakable desire before he gives a single, resolute nod. I hurry out of the room and into the guest bathroom, where I spot the first aid kit, finding a fresh pack of condoms inside with a bottle of lube beside it. Ignoring the rush of thoughts swirling in my mind, I grab both and return to the bedroom. Garred is stretched out on the bed, lying on his back, completely bare, waiting for me. His cock is thick and ready, his gaze locked onto mine with an intensity that sends a delicious shiver down my spine.

I straddle him, and Garred's hands move to prepare me, starting with one finger, then adding another, each stretch pulling a low moan from my throat. The buildup is slow, each passing minute heightening the anticipation between us. When I'm finally ready, he carefully rolls on a condom then slicks a generous amount of lube over it. I begin to ease down onto him, every inch filling me as we both moan, the intensity and stretch almost overwhelming. His hands grip my hips, holding still to give me a moment to adjust, and we breathe together, our skin hot and damp.

When I finally sink down, fully seated on him, Garred curses, his eyes squeezing shut, his breathing unsteady as he holds onto every ounce of control. I place my hands over his, feeling the tension in his grip on my hips, and begin to move—lifting myself slowly, then sliding back down, a wave of pleasure washing over me as he hits every perfect spot. Watching Garred unravel beneath me, his mouth slightly open, cheeks flushed, gives me a thrill of power. I want to hear him lose it, so I pick up the pace, rolling my hips faster. His grip tightens, and he starts meeting each of my movements, thrusting up to meet me, his rhythm driving us both to the edge.

Then his hand finds my cock, stroking in sync with each thrust, and I can't hold back, whimpering and moaning as I finally let go, climaxing in hot pulses across his chest. Seeing that seems to push Garred over the edge, too, and with one last moan, he grips my hips hard, pulsing as he comes inside me. We're both trembling, bodies pressed close, breaths ragged as the last waves of pleasure wash over us.

***

Light filters through the frost-feathered window, casting patterns across the bed that shift and dance with each passing cloud. I'm warm despite the winter chill—almost too warm, really, with Garred practically radiating heat behind me. His leg is hooked over mine possessively, and I can feel his heartbeat against my back, steady and strong.

"God, it's hot," I mumble, shifting restlessly against him.

"You know," he murmurs against my neck, his voice gravelly with sleep, "I've never actually had someone steal all the blankets and then complain about being too hot."

"I did not steal—" I start to protest, but then I notice that, yes, somehow, I've managed to cocoon myself in most of the comforter, leaving him with just a corner.

His laugh is soft and fond as he tugs at the blanket. "Share?"

I loosen my grip on the blanket, letting him pull some back

over himself as I turn to face him. The morning light catches his face just right, highlighting a small scar near his temple I hadn't noticed before. Without thinking, I reach up to trace it with my finger.

"Training accident," he explains, catching my hand and pressing a kiss to my palm. "First week at the academy. Turns out fire hoses are harder to control than they look."

I try to picture a younger, less muscular Garred struggling with equipment, but it's difficult to reconcile with the confident man I know. "Tell me more about that," I say, genuinely curious. "About being a firefighter."

He props himself up on one elbow, looking thoughtful. "It's not that interesting, you know. Mostly, it's preventive inspections, false alarms, and helping elderly ladies whose cats won't come down from trees."

"And here I thought you spent all day posing for calendars."

His eyes spark with amusement. "Only on Tuesdays."

We fall into a comfortable silence, just looking at each other. His hand finds its way to my hip, thumb tracing lazy circles that make my skin tingle. Everything feels soft and unhurried like we have all the time in the world.

"I like this," he says quietly.

"What?"

"Just...this. Waking up with you. Getting to touch you whenever I want." His fingers trail up my side, making me shiver. "Not having to pretend I'm not completely gone for you."

The simple honesty in his voice makes my heart flip. I lean in to kiss him, morning breath be damned, but before our lips meet, Mom's voice drifts up from downstairs:

"Breakfast is ready!"

I groan, dropping my forehead against Garred's chest. "She has absolutely tragic timing."

"At least she didn't install a baby monitor in here," Garred says with a wicked grin. "Though considering everything, I wouldn't put it past her."

"Don't even joke about that," I mutter, horrified at the possibility. "I'm already traumatized enough."

Another call drifts up from downstairs, and I yell back without thinking, "Five more minutes!"

I immediately regret it when Garred's eyebrows shoot up suggestively.

"Five minutes? That's ambitious. I need at least ten to properly appreciate—"

I silence him with a pillow to the face, but he just laughs and pulls me closer, morning stubble scratching deliciously against my neck. His hands wander lower, making me gasp.

"Never thought I'd be so grateful for Kelly's meddling," he murmurs against my skin.

"Less talking about Kelly," I manage, already breathless from his touch.

His laugh vibrates against my neck, but then his mouth finds mine, and suddenly, time becomes completely irrelevant.

We end up being very, very late for breakfast.

THE END

Author's Note

Thank you for purchasing this book! If you've enjoyed it, please consider leaving a review. Your feedback means the world to me and helps other readers discover the story.

Thank you for being part of this adventure!

Best wishes,
Gaia Tate

TikTok @authorgaiatate
Instagram @authorgaiatate
E-mail authorgaiatate@gmail.com

Made in United States
Cleveland, OH
28 September 2025